Also by the author:

*The Stars of Axuncanny* (novel)

# Dennis Dunkle on the Road (and Off)

## David Simms

**Livingston Press**
The University of West Alabama

UWA
The UNIVERSITY of
WEST ALABAMA

Hardcover binding by: HF Group
Typesetting and page layout: Sarah Coffey
proofreading: Barbara Anderson, Jayla Gellington, Erin Watt,
Joe Taylor
Cover layout: Joe Taylor
cover photo: David Simms

The author is indebted to Tom Aman, Bruce Chadwick, Laurine Kennedy, Rhonda Murray, Helen O'Rourke, Kathleen Petranech, Jane and Tim Radford, Joe Taylor, and Ginny Watson. And extra-extra indebted to Sheila Fletcher. Thank you so much, everyone. Bandit too. And Bennie and Shadow and Browni and Bluey. Earlier versions of portions of several chapters appeared as short stories in *Barbaric Yawp, The Greensilk Journal,* and *The Rejected Quarterly.* In Chapter Six, liberties have been taken with traditional accounts of a supposed plan to rescue Marie Antoinette from prison in France and whisk her to Ireland.

# Dennis Dunkle on the Road (and Off)

*for Gabriel*
*and for Gracie*

# PART I

# HERE

# ONE

There's the case of Myrtle Stefanowski. There are other cases. But Myrtle's is the one that Dennis Dunkle would bring up whenever Molly Minnelli was nagging him to join Amorous After Fifty. Myrtle's story had been on *29 Minutes*, one of a series of segments the program airs on disastrous outcomes of online dating matches.

*29 Minutes* is a production of Saint Plato Community College's journalism department and is shown on the college's very own television channel. It's often accused of making stuff up.

Dennis Dunkle was a librarian at the college until, well, barely a week ago when he resigned abruptly, though not surprisingly given his age and his random bouts of weirdness. Or maybe just his age. Librarians are expected to have random bouts of weirdness. He'd watched *29 Minutes* regularly, on a screen at his desk, as regularly at least as its irregular schedule would permit.

According to the program, Myrtle Stefanowski was an attractive widow who lived in a trailer park in Florida. She was said to have moved there from Hackensack after her husband's motorcycle stunt at his high school reunion went awry. She liked macho men but all she got in Florida were sweaty shuffleboard players. There were no crusty old men going out to sea anymore and bringing back big fish. So she joined Widows and Walruses and met Raymond Rooshig online. Raymond was a walrus poacher on Baffin Island. They got to doing Skype.

Myrtle was smitten. She ordered a parka from L.L. Bean, sold her trailer, and drove her old Mustang about as far north from Florida as one can drive. The car rattled to a halt on a dirt track in the Canadian bush alongside an old Piper Super Cub that was rattling in place. The pilot waved. Myrtle hired him to fly her the rest of the way to Baffin.

Raymond was in jail when she got there. Arrested for

1

walrus poaching. The third time. He was in deep walrus shit, as the program's narrator put it. Myrtle used up all the money she had left to bail him out. He took her to his cabin, administered some delightfully rough sex, announced he was going out for cigarettes, and never came back. Depressed and far from anywhere and out of money, Myrtle eventually doused herself with a can of walrus oil she found in the cabin and struck a match.

Of course, maybe the story was made up. But there were interviews with Myrtle's former neighbors at the trailer park—several of the journalism students had gone down to Florida on spring break and talked with them. And there was home-video footage of an ecstatic, Baffin-bound Myrtle showing off her new parka, getting into her old Mustang, blowing a kiss at the camera, and starting out. Footage of walruses too. And of a can of walrus oil. And of Raymond Rooshig's mug on a wanted poster the Mounties had distributed. He had something of a macho walrus look.

Dennis couldn't figure what women as lovely as Myrtle saw in men who looked like walruses. Or why men who looked like walruses would forsake women as lovely as Myrtle. Wasn't Raymond ever lonely?

Dennis was. Saint Plato had little to offer once he'd reach his daily quota of fantasies. And of surreptitious glances at coeds very much his junior cavorting in the library. In an incautious moment he did indeed join Amorous After Fifty. More like an incautious several hours, with Molly Minnelli's help, composing his profile, answering questions about himself, posting a photo of himself with his cat. Yet having done so, it was several months before he was in touch with anyone and then only because she was also from Saint Plato—although not the New Jersey Saint Plato where Dennis has spent most of his life but the North Dakota one, a place he hadn't heard of since grade school when fourth graders in the two Saint Platos wrote letters back and forth.

Such as that was. Dennis cared not a hoot about writing to some snot kid in North Dakota. What he did care about was gazing with fourth-grade lust at Gabriela Gloriosa's knees as

2

she stood in front of the class reading aloud her first letter to her new pen pal, Maria Cassatti.

Dennis got Olaf Olafsson.

*Dear Olaf,* he read to the class when it was his turn. *I am in the fourth grade. Yours truly, Dennis.*

His teacher tried to get him to write more but he couldn't bring himself to write more. Olaf didn't reply, which was fine with Dennis even though everyone else in the fourth grade received replies.

You should have listened to me, his teacher said to him after weeks had gone by and still there was no reply.

Dennis looked over at the empty desk where Gabriela Gloriosa used to sit. Her family had just moved away, unexpectedly, during the Thanksgiving holiday. To Valparaiso. Or Vancouver. Or Vladivostok for all he knew. He never did find out where. To Gabriela he would've written much more. But she was beyond gone. She and the guinea pigs and whatnots she'd bring to school for show and tell, and the balloons. Every day she'd bring in a balloon, tie it to her desk, watch it hover above her.

*

It's a few days past a much later Thanksgiving now, many decades later, and Dennis Dunkle is hunched over the steering wheel of his once shiny white Chrysler Cruiser, well-weathered and dented from New Jersey's sun and snow and salt air and savage parking lots, unlike the brand new, shiny white toilet that's strapped to the roof rack. Dennis's hands are clasped tightly onto the steering wheel. His knuckles are turning white. He's caught in a horrendous wide-awake nightmare on a maelstrom of an interstate loop he didn't mean to be on, circling Indianapolis, Indiana, vehicles jammed together, moving excessively fast on lanes narrowed by inscrutable road work.

A sign up ahead warns *Keep Right If You Know What's Good for You.* Dennis keeps right and finds himself on an improvised exit ramp. He and the Cruiser and the toilet and Sebastian, his cat, who trusts him implicitly to get them through this. The ramp winds this way and that until it comes to a red light.

At this moment Dennis knows he can't go back. It's as if he's been shot out of a wormhole and he can't go back through it. Ever. Which is okay. He doesn't want to go back.

The light turns green. Arrows direct him to more this ways and thats. Holding his breath, he chances ignoring the arrows, taking a that way and this instead, and comes to a gentler highway where he can begin to relax.

He pauses *La Bohème,* the CD of it that's been playing, that he's not been listening to, not even been aware of the last half hour. During the agony of the maelstrom, it played on to the third and fourth acts. He never intentionally plays those parts, the sad parts. Now on the gentler highway, he starts it at the beginning again, the first act, the happier act.

He'd never given opera much thought until Vietnam where he came by some LPs of the music. They'd belonged to a sergeant who went missing. Dennis took to listening to the vinyl and fantasizing that one or another diva would walk into his life and make everything right. A real diva like Maria Callas or a make-believe one, a Grace Slick or a Sylvia Tyson or someone, turned operatic.

The daydreams continued after the war. A brief interlude when he married Mirabelle and brought her back to Saint Plato after library school. But Mirabelle was a nightmare. And couldn't sing. And hated opera. Dennis resumed his fantasies and expanded them to include actresses in films he'd watch at the Bijou on Main Street.

*

Denise sings. She even was in an opera once. Denise is the woman in North Dakota that Dennis and Sebastian are going to spend the rest of their lives with, Denise and her cat. She visited Dennis's profile on Amorous After Fifty and dinged him. He noted the ding and the Saint Plato connection and the blank space where there was no photograph of herself and Tuffy.

4

He sent her a message. She wrote back, told him she'd skipped the fourth grade, skipped all of grade school in fact. And didn't have a library card. *I origamied it,* she wrote. No photographs either, she was an artist, a painter as a rule but she didn't follow rules and didn't believe in photographs. Maybe she looks like Michelle Pfeiffer in *The Fabulous Baker Boys* or like Andie MacDowell in *Four Weddings and a Funeral.* Dennis would just have to come and see. As for her cat, Tuffy looks just like a Tuffy should.

Dennis requested *The Fabulous Baker Boys* and *Four Weddings and a Funeral* from Netflix, movies he'd once seen at the Bijou, and he watched them again in his office in the college library, imagining Michelle Pfeiffer as Denise, Andie MacDowell as Denise. He was enthralled. Googling cats named Tuffy, no two looked alike.

He wrote to Denise that he and Sebastian would be delighted to come and see just exactly what she looks like and see which Tuffy Tuffy looks like too and accompany Denise to her library to get a new library card.

She replied that she didn't want a new library card, she only patronized used book stores now, no fussing about lost books, overdue books, paint-splattered books, books peed on by a cat, and why don't he and Sebastian just come and see permanently, just come live with her and Tuffy in North Dakota.

Pulse rate rocketing, Dennis went paging through a road atlas over in Reference, then stumbled back to his desk and called Denise for the first time.

*Amare o non amare* is how she answered her phone. To love or not to love.

Huh? Denise? This is Dennis Dunkle.

Oh. *To love* then! *Amare!* When are you getting here?

Uh. I —

He had to hang up, his heart was pounding. An emergency in Periodicals, he told her, he'd call back shortly. He went and peed and took deep breaths. When he did call back, he began to fabricate a missing set of art journals as the emergency, only to be interrupted by Denise. I used to have a pen pal from New Jersey, she said. Gabriela something-or-other. But she moved far away from there.

Gabriela Gloriosa? You were pen pals with Gabriela Gloriosa? Dennis said. Holy moly! She was in the fourth grade here.

If you say so.

But if you skipped grade school? I mean, how did you become pen pals?

Hmmm, Denise said. The details escape me.

Wait, Dennis said. Gabriela's pen pal was a girl named Maria Cassatti.

Oh that, she said. That was one of my aliases. She said she and Gabriela kept writing after the Gloriosas left New Jersey. For years they remained pen pals, though they never met. Gabriela became a veterinarian and flew a hot air balloon for sport. And then a note from her family. Gabriela and her balloon had gone missing. The worst was feared.

Dennis brushed away a tear, several. He confessed he'd had a crush on Gabriela. And he'd been crushed when she moved away. I've always wondered, he asked, where was it that she moved to?

I forget, Denise said. Maybe Venus. Listen, Dennis, life is short. You and me, this is fate. This is *destino!* Don't wait, come live with me. *Rapidamente! Immediatamente!*

You wouldn't like to meet first?

Why meet? *Destino* is *destino.* We will become *uno.*

Dennis was a goner, the case of Myrtle Stefanowski irrevocably overridden. Are you Italian? he asked.

*Intermittentemente,* she replied.

The next day on the phone he asked if she liked opera.

I had a part in Schicchi's *Gianni Puccini* in college, she said.

Don't you mean Puccini's *Gianni Schicchi?*

No.

The random mystery of her!

Shortly before he left for North Dakota, she told him her toilet was broken. I've constructed an outhouse in the backyard, she said. My first piece ever of interactive installation art! It's painted red. *Rosso.* In homage to Tiziano. That's Titian's original name, you know. Tiziano.

But winter was around the corner. Global warming notwithstanding, using an outhouse, any color outhouse, in North Dakota in winter, that would be fifty shades of frigid. Dennis picked out a shiny new toilet at the Saint Plato Home Depot, a tall, elongated American Standard, had a roof rack installed on the Cruiser, and had the toilet strapped on.

*

Their first night on the road, at a Happy Inn in Carnegie, Pennsylvania, Dennis turned on the television in their room to an *Inspector Montalbano* mystery. In Italian with English subtitles. When it was over, Sebastian yawned and Dennis tried to call Denise on his cell phone. He got a busy signal.

Dennis had tried calling when they checked in but got a busy signal then too, just like the night before when he wanted to say hello and goodbye for the last time from New Jersey. This time he was planning to say hello and goodbye for the only time from Pennsylvania and to tell Denise how Carnegie got its name. From Mr. Carnegie obviously. But there was more to it. A brochure in the room had the town making a deal with the man, renaming itself after him so it could get a library.

The Andrew Carnegie Free Library and Music Hall, a spectacular building more than a hundred years old. Dennis had hoped to visit it. He drove there before going to the motel, but the library was closing and he could only walk about the grounds and look in a window and tell Sebastian what he saw through the window.

*

Between Pennsylvania and Ohio, they stopped outside Wheeling, where Dennis's daughter Beverly lives, in that odd appendage of West Virginia that sticks up on a map. It was a courtesy call, dropping off her grandmother's ashes. Beverly wants everyone's ashes for the end time so that, after everyone's reconstituted, they can spend eternity shooting up the woods there. Like Dennis's granddaughters were doing as he pulled in.

He already knew it was a mistake, stopping. He hadn't seen Beverly in years and hoped the next time would be never. As he got out of the car, she shouted, Hey, you bringing us that toilet too? He had other plans for it, he said, and told her no more. She had a snit and shouted that if he had to pee, to climb up onto his car roof and use that toilet so his granddaughters would have a clear shot at him. Home-schooled, they kept yelling grammatical obscenities and were appallingly adept at shooting every which way. Sebastian stayed out of sight under the passenger seat.

Dennis and the cat were out of there in a New Jersey twinkle after one of the car's hubcaps got shot, Dennis's unvoiced *Up yours, Beverly,* hanging in the air behind them. Sebastian wouldn't stir from under the seat until the car had reached cruising speed and Dennis had fully exhaled and the prelude to *The Barber of Seville* had begun.

*

There wouldn't be a Sebastian in Dennis's life had his mother not croaked last year. She'd always intended to leave him out of her will but never got around to writing one. So he got the house. Molly Minnelli performed a cleansing ritual in it, burning sage, and he gave up his longtime room at the seedy Saint Plato Arms and moved in, adopting the cat first thing from the Saint Plato Animal Shelter.

He'd grown up in the house. As a young child, he'd ride his tricycle down the street to Mr. and Mrs. Baker's and play with their big white cat, Big Guy. He called Mr. Baker *Uncle Billy* but Mrs. Baker was always *Mrs. Baker.* They both were kind to him. Uncle Billy was a carpenter and Mrs. Baker taught second grade.

Her first year of teaching, Mrs. Baker had Dennis's mother in the second grade, though she was hardly Dennis's mother yet of course. She did not get along with the other children in the class. Mrs. Baker would send her home with a note. She would be sent back with another note:

*She doesn't get along with anyone at home either. Can't you just keep her in a corner or something?*

Her parents died, somewhat suspiciously, a cause never determined, when she was an adolescent. She finagled her way from aunt to aunt, inheriting a tidy bundle when she came of age.

When Dennis would get home from playing with Big Guy at Mr. and Mrs. Baker's, his mother would start sneezing. The more she sneezed, the more she hated cats. The more she hated cats, the more she hated Dennis, although she already hated him a lot. She tried to poison him once, he was three, but the hot dog smelled funny to him.

New type of hot dog. Eat! she demanded.

He dumped it into the trash.

Go to bed hungry then, you little freak!

*

Dennis's and Mirabelle's own house backed up to Saint Plato Creek and when Beverly was five he brought home a kitten for her from the animal shelter. But like his mother, his wife Mirabelle hated cats. And hated Dennis. She smirked at the kitten and encouraged Beverly to be rough with it. The next day Dennis came home early to check on it and spotted Beverly dragging a sack toward the creek.

What's this? he yelled, alarmed, hurrying up to her.

What do you think it is? Beverly said as she reached the creek. Mommy says kittens are better off drowned. Dennis wrestled the sack from her.

I hate you, Beverly shouted, just like Mommy does. Mirabelle came outside then and had a tantrum to illustrate the point.

He took the kitten back to the shelter.

*

Dennis moved to the Saint Plato Arms after Mirabelle tried to poison him herself, an omelet she made from mushrooms she and Beverly had gathered along the creek.

9

He never quite accumulated the amount of dauntless superhuman resolve that would have been required to get through a divorce from her. Moving out was bad enough, a screech here, a screech there. Divorcing her, she'd have screeched at him the whole way. Inexplicable, given that she hated him, but she would have, he knew she would have. Scornful, debasing screeches. And she'd have trashed the college library.

He'd finished his BA and gotten a library degree after Vietnam, the GI bill. He and Mirabelle met in library school. His BA was in philosophy, a synchronicity with Denise who had also studied philosophy.

Denise's appearance in *Gianni Puccini* was just for fun, she said. And she still sings for fun while she paints. Gianni jingles, she calls them. Denise sang Gianni jingles while painting the outhouse, sings them while painting self-portraits on the walls in her house, sang them after the beep on Dennis's library voice mail.

He didn't tell anyone about the omelet. Nor about Mirabelle trying to run him over with a battered pickup truck. Who would believe him? Mirabelle didn't have a battered pickup truck. Or any pickup truck. A few weeks later she crashed the battered truck, or one just like it, into the creek. She'd been seen trying to run over a cat. She's in a coma at Saint Plato General.

Dennis fears that to seek a divorce even now would not be safe. Mirabelle would rise up screeching from her coma. Likewise, if he gave his consent to remove life support, what the doctors have been advising. So he's handed over to Mirabelle's sister the power to unplug her. He's explained this to Denise. She made the equivalent on the phone of what a shrug would be.

\*

Halfway to North Dakota, in a Happy Inn in Danville, Illinois, propped on pillows on the bed, Dennis is looking at his maps, trying to figure out Indianapolis, what happened there. He can't. He turns on the television and comes across a rerun of the *Inspector Montalbano* mystery he watched in Carnegie. Sebastian is working over what's left of the veggie burgers and the slice of sweet potato pie Dennis brought back to the room from the Big Guy Veggie Café across the road. For the trip, he'd filled a miniature sports bag, a promotional item from the First Bank of Saint Plato, with cans of Sebastian's favorite cat food. But tonight the cat gets veggie fare.

Framed photographs of Danville natives Gene Hackman and Dick Van Dyke and Donald O'Connor were on the wall just inside the entrance to the Big Guy Veggie Café. Standing next to the photographs, waiting for his order, Dennis fantasized that the café was named after the Bakers' cat. Last he heard, the Bakers were having their living assisted for them in Vineland, in a facility a grandniece had moved them to, subsisting on hot meatloaf sandwiches no doubt. But they'd be well over 100 now and most likely dead. Their Big Guy is long dead. He did survive a suspected poisoning once.

When the *Inspector Montalbano* rerun ends, Dennis picks up his cell phone and calls Denise's number. There's no answer. Nor does her voice on her answering machine greet him with its *Buongiorno! If you wish to speak with me, deposit ten billion lire for the first light year per favore.*

Denise did answer the night before when he called her from a Happy Inn in Zanesville, Ohio. But she said she couldn't talk, she was in the middle of giving Tuffy a philosophy quiz. The night before that and the night before the night before that, Tuffy had been online looking up the philosopher Derrida's cat to prepare for the quiz, she said, thus the busy signals. Denise has dial-up.

Last night in Zanesville Dennis wanted to tell her about Zane Grey and Colonel Ebenezer Zane, about which got named after which. And more. But with Denise in the middle of Tuffy's quiz, he couldn't.

Tonight he wanted to tell her about Gene Hackman and Dick Van Dyke and Donald O'Connor. And ask if Tuffy uses a litter box like Sebastian. Or does Tuffy go outside like Denise?

\*

When Dennis first saw Sebastian at the animal shelter, the cat was burrowed behind a crumpled towel in his cage. Attached to the door of the cage, this note:

*Hello, my name is Sebastian. I'm fixed and I'm eccentric.*

Sebastian had the most expressive and inquisitive blue eyes and the whitest fluffy white fur. He was bigger even than Big Guy had been. When Dennis said hello, the cat wiggled the tip of his tail and made a muffled sound, a soft *irrrph,* as he peeked over the towel with his expressive, inquisitive blue eyes.

Their first night together, when Dennis got into bed, Sebastian curled up next to his face, purring. A soothing purr. A soothing smell to his fur as well. When Dennis rolled over in the middle of the night, the cat got up and crossed behind the pillow and settled on the other side so that he'd still be next to Dennis's face.

In the morning, Sebastian hopped into the shower with him. No wimpy waiting around, like Derrida's cat, for Dennis to emerge from the shower so the cat could stare at him. He hopped right in and stared.

Today, after they left Zanesville, it rained through most of Ohio and Sebastian seemed utterly enchanted by the rain falling on the windshield, the wipers swooshing the water back and forth. He lay on his back, paws in the air, watching, spellbound.

Back in New Jersey, on a day trip all the way up to the Ikea in Elizabeth, Molly Minnelli along, endeavoring to be his decorator, Dennis had gotten new furnishings for the entire house, most of the stuff with Sebastian in mind. When it was delivered, he fixed cozy little Camelots in room after room for the cat to slumber in or to look out at the world from. He'd already picked up a handsome water fountain at a pet supply place, and a handsome litter box and biodegradable litter and a slicker brush. At a craft fair he happened upon on a back road, he found a beautiful sisal scratching post and a handmade toy hedgehog.

Molly had kept nagging him about Amorous After Fifty. Your mother's dust, your wife's a vegetable, they both tried to kill you, she said one day on their way to Trader Joe's. Sebastian was low on cat food and Molly wanted to check out a checkout girl. You're in love with a cat for chrissake!

Another woman might also try to kill me, Dennis said.

So look for a guy, Molly bantered.

Dennis bantered back that card catalogs would make a comeback first.

Molly's gay. She fantasizes she's married to Liza Minnelli. She and Dennis have known each other since grade school. She was in the fourth grade with him and also had a crush on Gabriela Gloriosa.

Pulling into Trader Joe's parking lot, Dennis asked, How could I be certain of any woman I'd meet online? That she wouldn't be homicidal?

We'll make it a stipulation, Molly said.

When he finally capitulated, she monitored. That photo sucks, she said of the one he was about to post on the site. She took a new photo of him with Sebastian. She had him begin his profile with *I'm seeking a woman who won't try to kill me.*

*

Dennis and his unwed mother met for the first time outside the womb on the Fourth of July. *Nine months and I get one with a thingy hanging between its legs,* Gladys Dunkle wrote in his baby book. Every Fourth of July, on into his teens, she'd throw a firecracker into his bedroom to wake him on his birthday.

His unwed father skipped before the birth. That's what his mother said. Dennis couldn't blame him and, besides, he likes the name FitzSweeney. If that really is his father's name. He has only his mother's word.

Once he rode his bicycle the whole three miles out Atlantic Avenue to FitzSweeney Wash and Fold. He was maybe nine, maybe in the third grade. The place was run by a Chinese family named FitzSweeney. They just grinned and nodded, neither a *yes* nod nor a *no* nod, when he inquired whether he might be related to them. They knew no English, it seemed, and looked nothing like him. He never told his mother about the excursion.

And he's never much trusted her word, she who was habitually mean and untruthful and prone to farfetchedness. *Dear Fraulein Dunkel,* a worn letter he found in her effects began. *We are not in a position to make an offer at this time but dankeschön for your note on the availability of the Brooklyn Bridge. Sincerely, Die Schutzstaffel.*

Possibly her own forgery, yet provocative with Dunkle spelled *Dunkel,* the German way.

\*

The first act of *Carmen* is playing as they make their way past Urbana, as they make their way past Champaign. As they cross the bridge over the Illinois River in Peoria, Sebastian stands with his front paws on the sill of the passenger window, gazing down at the river. Later, from the Spoon River bridge, there's not much river to see. But in another hour or so, the wide, wide Mississippi, Dennis amazed at how wide it is, Sebastian beside himself, hopping from window to window, peering at it.

Then Iowa City. Which is where Sebastian starts hiccupping. Hiccup after hiccup after hiccup. The cat hiccups right up to the Iowa City Happy Inn, right into their room.

Dennis tries to get him to hold his breath but he doesn't catch on. He just stares at Dennis and hiccups. There's no paper bag in the room for him to breathe into, if even he would, and Dennis doesn't want to try to scare him out of the hiccups.

Denise might know what to do, but she's not answering her phone again. Nor is her answering machine answering. Denise whatever-her-last-name. She won't tell. Maybe it's Dunkle, she teased when he asked last week. He'd called to let her know he'd bought the toilet. So after we get married, she said, I'll be Dunkle-hyphen-Dunkle. Or Dunkle-minus-Dunkle. She was giggling. Dunkle-minus-Dunkle-minus-Dunkle-minus-Dunkle-minus-Dunkle. Elongated like our new toilet. My name might not fit anywhere. The toilet might not fit anywhere. My bathroom is odd.

Not as odd as Dennis's mother's bathroom. It couldn't be. His mother had kept a poison ivy plant by the sink. And a pile of wet movie magazines on a shelf next to the bathtub. He remembers Janet Leigh in something plunging on the cover of one of the magazines. And then that magazine was gone. It was around the time Gabriela Gloriosa moved away. For solace, he went to borrow an art book from the Saint Plato Public Library, an oversize volume on modern art, but the librarian wouldn't let him. You're too young for nudes descending staircases, she reproached.

Sebastian hiccups all night, is still hiccupping in the morning. Dennis looks up veterinarians in the yellow pages. One listing leaps out at him, a clinic called Gabriela's.

There's no answer when he tries to phone for an appointment so he just drives to the address with his hiccupping cat. But there's no clinic at the address. No Gabriela of any sort. The place is a hypnotist's office. The hypnotist looks like Gwyneth Paltrow in *Sliding Doors*. Her name is Denise. She's never heard of a Gabriela's Veterinary Clinic.

Dennis tells her of his Denise. He tells Denise that Denise hasn't been answering her phone.

Watch out for us Denises, she says.

She hypnotizes Sebastian. When you wake up, you will no longer hiccup, she tells him.

And when Sebastian wakes up, he no longer hiccups. They celebrate. Denise rolls a joint for her and Dennis, sprinkles a little on the floor for Sebastian. The cat rolls and rolls in it. Dennis inhales deeply, feels instantly mellow. He hasn't smoked in years. He brought back a bag, several bags, from Vietnam, smoked sparingly. In one of her rampages, Mirabelle dumped what was left into the creek.

This isn't marijuana, Denise says.

It's not?

Nope. It's corn husks. I hypnotize them into thinking they're weed.

Pleasantly numb, Dennis and Sebastian go back to the Happy

15

Inn for another night. In the morning, back to Denise's office for some hypnotized husks for the road. But the hypnotist's sign is gone, the hypnotist is gone, the place is empty.

*

On the road again, under a clear late autumn Iowa sky. Cornfield after cornfield reduced to stubs of stalks. Vestiges of unhypnotized husks. *Falstaff* playing, Verdi's comic opera. Sebastian being himself as if he'd never hiccupped, playing with his toy hedgehog.

Signs along the highway announce *Avenue of the Saints*. A curious name. In a lounge at a truck stop near Waterloo, Iowa, Dennis asks an old salt of a truck driver with a pony tail about it. Beats the bejesus out of me, the truck driver says.

The cap he's wearing, the name *FitzSweeney's Trucking* is printed on it. Dennis inquires, is told the cap was lying around at a truck stop in Montana. All the while, the driver's counting little blue pills, a big pile of them. I've enough of these babies for trysts all the way to Mars and back, he says.

How'd you get so many? Dennis asks.

Yard sales in Nebraska, the driver says.

Dennis has his own stash—a windfall from Freddy Gonzalez-Schmidt, his doctor in New Jersey. A peculiar fellow. Some days you'd see him skateboarding along Main Street. Some days he'd speak only in Spanish. Or in *Achtung*s. He also dispensed legendary amounts of free samples. There were men in Saint Plato who kept an eye out year-round for the Viagra rep's car to pull up outside his office. Dennis wasn't one of them but he had a checkup before leaving for North Dakota that happened to coincide with the rep's visit—a tall smug-looking woman wearing a shiny suit and knee-high boots and wheeling a large satchel.

Freddy gave Dennis all the samples. He hadn't asked for any but he'd told the doctor about Denise. It had been a very long time since Mirabelle and no one since. You might need jump starts, Freddy said. All those geezers salivating in the waiting room—*Hola! Auf Wiedersehen!*—they can go boink on

16

their own tonight. He had Dennis leave by a back door.

*

Mirabelle hadn't been a student at library school, hadn't gone to college even. She was a secretary in the school's office. She pegged Dennis the day he showed up to register. Her boyfriend liked to watch kung fu movies on late night television after sex and she figured she would come up in the world, sleeping with someone who maybe would watch Dick Cavett after sex, though she didn't understand Dick Cavett. She left an anonymous note in Dennis's student mailbox, that her knees went weak every time she saw him. Not true exactly, or partly for that matter, but so what?

Dennis went around frustrated, unable to figure who might have written the note. Mirabelle primped obsessively, plotting for him to ask if the note was from her. He didn't. After a week she sat down next to him in the school's cafeteria. I can't go another step, she sighed, my knees are weak. That night they conceived Beverly, somehow, halfway under the ragged tonneau cover of his ramshackle Triumph Spitfire that had belonged to Molly Minnelli's brother. Mirabelle turned the radio on after but got static.

He might have loved her at the beginning, a day here, a day there. Dutifully married, Beverly on the way, he tried hard. But Mirabelle wasn't easy to love. And she never did come up in the world. Dennis let her down, it seemed, not being inclined to watch any television after sex. After a few years, after he had his library degree and the position back home at the community college, Mirabelle herself started watching kung fu movies late at night in a separate bedroom after no sex. Dennis started going out late, to the Saint Plato Diner where Molly was waitressing—she's manager now— or to the library though it was closed. He had a key. And an understanding with campus security.

17

*

He's bringing little with him. Enough clothes, Sebastian's food and pillows and water fountain and sisal scratching post and litter box and slicker brush and toy hedgehog, the CDs of operas that he grabbed on his way out the door the morning he left, the Viagra, a jug of Veezlaat, the illegal grog distilled in Saint Plato. Molly will pack his books and stuff, the rest of his clothes, and ship them later, whatever he decides he wants, whatever he and Denise decide they want. Molly's been sharing his house with him. She might buy it. They've talked about it.

But Dennis's vision of sweet bliss in North Dakota is getting less clear with each passing *Avenue of the Saints* sign, each unanswered phone call. He tries again without success at the Minnesota Welcome Center. The sky's still clear, still late autumny, the temperature not bad. On a table inside the building are posters for the taking of Minnesota scenes. He takes one of the Twins celebrating winning their first World Series.

Dennis had concluded by boot camp that the odds were against his becoming a famous baseball player. He hadn't been to library school yet or quite finished his BA but, assuming he made it back from Vietnam, life as a librarian seemed more likely. Growing up, he would write pretend information about pretend books on index cards. He had a drawerful of them, arranged by the Dennis Decimal System.

He also had a drawerful of pretend baseball cards he made of himself. Back then, he would listen to Jersey City Giants and Newark Bears games on the radio. He'd fantasize making a spectacular catch for the final out in the World Series, robbing the other team of a home run and the title. As spectacular a catch as the ones the announcer would describe Monte Irvin making out in left field for Jersey City before being called up by the New York Giants. Dennis sent away for a poster of Monte Irvin and put it up on his bedroom wall.

Ha. A thingy between your legs and a Negro on the wall,

his mother scoffed.

The poster's still there, though torn. His mother was found on the floor by it after her stroke, a piece of it clutched in her hand.

*

Dennis finds a Happy Inn a few exits beyond the Minnesota Welcome Center and checks in. He gives Sebastian a can of Tantalizing Turbot and a good brushing, makes a few more unanswered phone calls, and eats two pickled eggs and a giant pretzel from the Waterloo truck stop. He reads aloud to Sebastian, brochures about the Spam Museum nearby, about other local diversions, until he falls asleep. Sebastian fusses with the brochures, rearranging them with his paws.

The next day—a day of truth, Dennis believes, Dennis fears—and the Avenue of the Saints has veered off the wrong way. Dennis veers onto a less travelled road that will take him toward North Dakota's Saint Plato, him and Sebastian and *Porgy and Bess.*

It's sunny, but this far north this time of year the sun is low in the sky all day. Beyond Montevideo, Minnesota, and its two rivers, it half blinds him as he passes a church, perhaps the church where Denise had a commission to paint a large portrait of Saint Denise. One of the Saint Denises anyway, she said, there are lots of us. A sun-blighted image of a sign in front of the church catches a corner of Dennis's eye. Did it say *Saint Denise's?* He drives back. It did. Into the church they go, Sebastian over to the holy water font for a long drink, Dennis up the nave to the altar where a very large portrait dominates. This Saint Denise looks like Kate Winslett in *Eternal Sunshine of the Spotless Mind.*

Farther along, almost to North Dakota, the Cruiser's gas gauge bottoms out. Dennis hadn't been paying attention. Not like him. Alarmed, he barely makes it to a Casey's. He fills the tank, goes inside, buys a few bananas. The clerk looks like Scarlett Johansson in *Lost in Translation.* Her name tag says *Denise.*

Heading back to the car, Dennis spots a lottery ticket on the ground, discarded no doubt, a loser. But no. It's for Minnesota's Gopher 5 drawing tonight. Its numbers match Denise's phone number. Buoyed, he tries calling her once more. She doesn't answer. Her answering machine doesn't answer.

Sebastian sniffs the lottery ticket and goes *irrrph* when Dennis shows it to him in the car. If it's a winner, the prize money would have to be claimed back here in Minnesota. But it won't be a winner, Dennis never wins anything. Matching Denise's phone number like it does, it'll be a souvenir.

A delivery van with the lettering *FitzSweeney's Cupcakes* pulls in next to the Cruiser and the driver gets out with a tray of cupcakes. Lowering his window, Dennis calls to him, Are you Mr. FitzSweeney?

Nah, he says. It's a made-up name, you know. Exotic like. Hey, your license plate? You brought that toilet all the way from New Jersey?

Uh, Dennis says. It's for a contest.

No kidding? I've got an extra toilet at home. Do you think—?

Too late really. The results are being announced today.

Ah, shucks. Well, good luck. I hope you win.

Minnesotans are breeds apart. That sergeant in Vietnam, the one with the LPs of operas who went missing, he was from Bemidji. He had a toilet shipped to him, a top-of-the-line Kohler which he set over a hole in the ground near the perimeter of the base. He'd sit on it and read old issues of *Opera News*. Just after what turned out to be his and Dennis's last game ever of honeymoon bridge, the second act of *Pagliacci* playing in full smoldering timbre, the sergeant walked off toward the toilet. Before he reached it, a mortar round struck. The toilet was destroyed.

The sergeant's mind went missing. He kept walking and the rest of him went missing. The mortar round was from friendly fire. Dennis missed the bridge games.

Denise played bridge in college. She'd only bid hearts and diamonds. She also had a chess set with red pieces on both sides. That way if you're red, you always win, she reasoned.

Dennis tried playing chess growing up but calculating moves in advance made him anxious and he got to hate the game and played no more. Molly Minnelli also had no use for chess, and she and Dennis concocted a tall tale once about a fictitious chess championship in Saint Plato, the principals snuffed out, a bit of Saint Plato noir.

When she was still answering her phone, Denise said she might paint the new toilet red. Also in homage to Tiziano. Like her red chess set. Like her red outhouse. Like her red front door. That's how he could easily find her house, just look along her street for a red front door.

# TWO

Back when his mother croaked, back before there were any Denises in Dennis's life, or any red front doors, he had Funk's Funeral Home cremate the remains. Those weren't Gladys Dunkle's ashes he dropped off at his daughter Beverly's in West Virginia though. They weren't anyone's. What Beverly got was an urnful of wood chips, a sprinkling of aquarium gravel mixed in. Not in the original urn either.

The real ashes Dennis dumped into Saint Plato Creek. Float away, float away, float away all, he chanted, or sink for all I care, flinging the original urn into the creek as well. It wasn't far from the spot where his wife Mirabelle would crash a battered pickup truck into the creek and become a vegetable.

Dennis ignored Beverly's demands for the ashes he didn't have. And she wouldn't come to New Jersey for them, which worked out just fine considering. But then North Dakota happened and Beverly's was on the way and Dennis improvised. Molly Minnelli thought it a lark. A new urn was ordered from Funk's and Gracious Funk swung open the funeral home's bronze-tinted door with its little oval window when Dennis went to pick it up.

Gracious actually swung open the door before Dennis got to it and out strutted Silas Punterponk, Saint Plato's oldest living gentleman lecher. A barmy affluent gadabout to boot, affluent by way of old money.

Are you bereaved? he asked Dennis.

Uh, no. I—

Out with it, well-met fellow.

Uh, well, I'm picking up an urn for a fellow librarian who wants to, uh, preserve the ashes from his deceased card catalog.

How randomly weird, Silas replied and strutted off.

Gracious waved goodbye to him and went and fetched the new urn. A while since Dennis had seen her.

Silas was making arrangements? he asked when she returned and handed him the urn. She'd made it herself, *Funk's*

*Funerals* etched on the bottom.

Arrangements? Oh. No, she giggled. No arrangements. Mr. Punterponk just stopped by to chat me up. And with her practiced, not-so-innocent innocent look, like Sharon Stone in *Basic Instinct,* or maybe like some other actress in some other film, she asked, That celestial fellow, is he still on your office wall?

Dennis blushed. Johannes Kepler? I guess so. I left him there. I've resigned. I'm moving away. I'll be living in Saint Plato, North Dakota.

Hmmm, she said. Saint Plato once, Saint Plato twice, going, going, gone. A mischievous smile and she pulled her shirt up with a flourish. She wasn't wearing anything underneath, just like that day in his office years ago.

Dennis's blush deepened. Uh—

For old time's sake, she giggled, holding the pose, then pulled her shirt back down and murmured, Flashes to ashes, and softly closed the door.

*

Silas Punterponk almost lost all his old money one recent summer, a midsummer night's nightmare in the making, after meeting a bogus inamorata online through Gentleman Lechers Seeking Inamoratas and Vice Versa. A con artist with an aptitude for cleaning out barmy affluent gadabouts, the bogus one herself gadded about Silas's mattress, unstuffing it of his affluency. But the mattress started feeling funny to him, lumps were missing, and he found her out, recovered the lumps, and threw her out.

I wasn't heartless though, Silas told Dennis one night in Fedankgo's Saloon. Not me. I'm a *gentleman* lecher. And she did have a certain charm. I gave her bus fare back to South Carolina and a little extra. She talked of reforming, of opening a geisha booth at a Walmart in Walterboro.

*29 Minutes* wanted to interview Silas but he refused, told them he'd copyrighted the experience for his memoirs.

23

Gracious's brother, Ignatius, founded the funeral home. Their father, Chuck Funk, was a birdboy in his youth at the town's now-defunct badminton tournaments from which Silas Punterponk repeatedly strutted away with the singles title. Chuck went on to study physics at Princeton and waylay famous physicists outside the Institute for Advanced Study with questions about time travel. He returned to Saint Plato and taught physics at the community college until he disappeared.

Ignatius is no longer around either. He's dead. A certain Mr. Edgarty came out of retirement and took over after Ignatius's departure. Mr. Edgarty still calls it Funk's. Gracious lives in the flat upstairs with her precocious kid and a woman from Scotland obsessed with embalming.

Before it became Funk's, it was just an old empty house, a large, imposing old empty house, mind you, but still an old empty house. Though more than that for Dennis. Gabriela Gloriosa had lived in it. He'd ride his bicycle past. Then the moving van. Eventually another family. But it was empty again and on the market when Ignatius, undertaker boards passed, apprenticeship completed, and in the throes of indecision, came across an extraordinary ad. An undertaker over in the Kittatinny Mountains, the very same Mr. Edgarty in fact, was retiring and selling his entire stock—hearse, embalming equipment, some leftover coffins, what have you.

Ignatius consulted his mother, Ithy Funk, who was in real estate, then got in touch with the man, and in no time he and Gracious were barreling toward the Kittatinnys in a Fedankgo Rent-a-Truck. Arriving at the prospective point of sale just as the elder undertaker's final funeral was proceeding to the cemetery, Ignatius and Gracious followed, paid their respects at graveside, then returned to Mr. Edgarty's funeral home to inspect the items. Ignatius was delighted with everything. A future full of funerals was at hand. He relinquished the certified check his mother had provided him with, the truck was loaded, and brother and sister barreled home, Gracious flooring it in the hearse.

Mr. and Mrs. Edgarty wasted no time making final preparations for a much longer barreling, all the way to Myrtle Stefanowski's neck of the woods in Florida—though there's no indication they ever crossed paths with her—where they purchased a modest condominium apartment and where they soon would find themselves missing New Jersey and their former way of life while sweating in Florida's oppressive heat and humidity. For want of anything else stimulating to do in that godforsaken climate, they would begin attending funerals in the area, of which there were many.

In Saint Plato, Ithy Funk made an offer on her son's behalf on the large, imposing old empty house. A stone's throw from several of the community's larger churches, it was the perfect location for a funeral home if there ever was one. The sale moved quickly from pending to a done deal and in a few months, renovations completed and the health department's inspection passed with flying colors, Funk's Funeral Home was open for business, ready for its first customer. That happened to be, after a couple of weeks wait, the county coroner who had an unclaimed body on his hands that had been found along the banks of Saint Plato Creek.

Ignatius treated it like a regular funeral, with viewing hours and a service right in the front parlor. Dennis didn't attend but a surprising number of people did, Silas Punterponk among them, more to see what Ignatius had done with the place than to view the deceased whom no one wanted to have known anyway and who certainly was not from Saint Plato. Gracious served an off-brand of champagne.

A letter to the editor of the *Weekly Banner,* name withheld on request, complained: *The whole sordid shebang for this unknown and unfortunate derelict who washed up on our shores was entirely inappropriate and indecent.* Anonymous letters began pouring in on both sides of the issue, most of those supporting the shebang suspected to have been written by Ignatius himself and by Gracious and Ithy, multiple versions from each.

That it was two weeks before Funk's had any customer at all might have been attributed to a lull in dying in Saint Plato. Not to mention an overabundance of undertaking establishments in the town already, six in fact if you count Widdowick's, although old Walt Widdowick would do funerals only on Wednesdays which didn't suit a lot of people.

More to the point, Ignatius was thought odd by most Saint Platoans, not someone they especially wanted to entrust with their dead.

Funk's Funeral Home? Ignatius's place? Over my dead body! Gladys Dunkle is said to have huffed into her phone once, the caller, said to have been Gracious, soliciting pre-arrangements.

Mirabelle once told Dennis that a teenage Ignatius had sidled up to her in Frozen Foods at the Shop Rite and fondled her. It was during one of her tantrums that she told him that. I liked it! she screeched. I wanted him to keep fondling. But I had to swat him for appearances.

Not just Ignatius, the whole Funk family is in the odd column. For starters, all of them are gaunt, though Dennis has always thought of Gracious as svelte. Chuck Funk was a gaunt kid obsessed with time travel who grew up to be a gaunt physics teacher who failed to show up after lunch one day to monitor his afternoon physics lab. Also not returning from lunch that day was Mrs. Rizzo from the admissions office. Rumor had it that Chuck had been building an odd-looking machine, also now missing, in the college's maintenance garage. Neither he nor Mrs. Rizzo has been heard from since.

Ithy is Greek, *Ithy* short for Ithaki, the Ionian island on which she was born and after which she was named. She and Chuck met when he was rambling about on it the summer after his graduation from Princeton. A timeless time, he called it. Since Chuck disappeared, Ithy's been wearing black designer shawls and speaking Greek a lot, to herself and to anyone else who will listen whether they understand it or not, creating an eccentric air about her. But, by blood or by marriage, once a Funk, always a Funk, and Ithy has always been in disgrace anyway what with the way she's raised her children.

26

As an adolescent, Gracious was observed more than once dancing barefoot in the aisles of the old J.C. Penney store on Main Street, waving a lace valance from Domestics over her head, one of those modern dances, it looked like, and you wouldn't know what sort of meaning it might have. If she's so much above it all, the consensus ran later on, why isn't she at Princeton, now that they're letting girls in, studying how to disappear for good like her father?

But for Dennis, Gracious has always been beyond reproach, even her not-so-innocent innocent look. He couldn't see her clearly, though, that day she walked unannounced into his office in the library. She was a student volunteer and he coordinated the volunteers. Hi, Mr. Dunkle, she said. I've a few minutes before class. Standing in front of his desk, facing him, she pulled off her shirt. She was wearing nothing underneath. You can look but you can't touch, she said.

Dennis was working on fiction acquisitions and had his reading glasses on and she was a little blurred. Uh—

He started to reach for his regular glasses but pulled his hand back. That wouldn't have been cool. He started to stand but that wouldn't have been cool either. He was becoming aroused. He sat back down. Gracious! I mean, Ms. Funk. I—

What does one say? What if someone walks by? They had barely spoken, ever, except for her interview, her duties, once about her courses. Please, I—

Dennis couldn't come up with a complete sentence, a complete thought. Gracious remained motionless, topless, apparently looking directly at him, apparently waiting for him to complete a sentence. Or a thought. He looked, then looked away, then snuck a look back again. Out of focus, yes, but nonetheless.

Would you like to see more? she asked, hands on hips.

No, Dennis whispered, meaning it. Not meaning it.

Time's almost up.

Uh—

Suddenly *Eeek!* Gracious quickly crossed her arms over her breasts, taking in for the first time a poster on the wall to one side of Dennis's desk. Who's that? she demanded, staring at the face in the poster.

Dennis glanced at it, looked back at Gracious, looked away, looked back. That's Johannes Kepler, he said. I —

He's been watching the whole time, Gracious interrupted. I —

Never mind. She grabbed her shirt, pulled it back on. I'll be late for class. She turned to leave.

He's known as the father of celestial mechanics, Dennis said.

The whole time, Gracious said, glancing back, then she was gone.

No one had walked past. No one had seen. Dennis sat numb at his desk. What had she been up to? She was not known to go out on dates. Her brother had escorted her to her senior prom in high school, there was talk.

Gracious continued her volunteer work in the library the rest of the semester. She was good at it, never missed a day. She acted like nothing had happened. The several times Dennis needed to speak with her, he tried to speak naturally. But he lived the moment over and over in fear, in guilt, in confusion, in excitement.

Years later when his mother croaked, excitement lingered. He might have arranged for the cremation with another funeral home. But he didn't. He might have ordered the new urn elsewhere. But he didn't.

*

Like his father, Ignatius had been quite gaunt. But he was not unhandsome, just as Gracious was far from unpretty. Yet he never seemed to go out on dates either, except for that senior prom, escorting his sister. In the years between his own graduation from high school and his first semester at the Day of the Dead Floating School of Mortuary Science offshore near Perth Amboy, he had frittered away much seed money from his mother, pursuing ill-advised business schemes, schemes he'd see advertised on matchbook covers. Why he wanted to go into undertaking was unknown, perhaps the idea came from another matchbook cover, but no one thought it out of character.

Besides converting the downstairs of the old house into a funeral home, Ignatius had the upstairs made into a comfortable flat. He and Gracious had always lived with their mother—and their father until he disappeared with Mrs. Rizzo—in a grand house over on East Avenue where many of Saint Plato's grand houses are. He drove to and from the mortuary school pier each day and to and from his apprenticeship in Toms River. But now, as proprietor of Funk's Funeral Home with its large sign with skinny letters out front that Gracious had painted, Ignatius left the nest and moved into the flat.

Gracious followed. She rarely used makeup herself and her courses at the community college had not included cosmetology, which wasn't taught there in any case, but she prodded Ignatius into letting her become the funeral home's cosmetician. She took up pottery as well and began making urns.

Business went from terrible to could be worse to slowly improving. Then Gracious got pregnant. She was almost due before anyone knew. Months of speculation were thereby avoided, including whether it happened before or after Leelagh Bobowicz moved into the flat and what that might have had to do with anything.

Leelagh Bobowicz, née Laird, had arrived in town the year before with her PhD husband, Ben Bobowicz, newly appointed assistant professor of English at the college. Researching wee little mousies, for all anyone knew, for his dissertation, he'd proposed to her in the provincial library where she worked in Scotland. Leelagh said yes, banking on a fairytale life in America. But after settling in Saint Plato in a house sold to them by Ithy Funk, she decided that if life in America was anything, it was boring. Ben seemed disappointing in bed to boot, not that she'd ever had anyone to compare him with.

How she became fascinated with funeral homes, or at least with Funk's, was never entirely clear. There were the several intriguingly odd conversations with Ignatius when he wandered into Fedankgo's Used Books, her new place of employment, and went paging through old undertaking magazines. Then, out of the blue, her posing a question about embalming. And Ignatius inviting her to watch. And within days her announcing to Ben that she was leaving him and moving in with Ignatius and Gracious, into the flat above the funeral home.

Ben was flattened. He staggered out of the house and on downtown to Fedankgo's Saloon and got very drunk and had to cancel his classes the next day.

Leelagh anticipated expanding her horizons, romping around the funeral home, trying her hand at a little embalming, and having a wee bit of you know what with Skinny Iggy Undertaker, as she grew fond of calling him. She ignored Ben's phone messages and the photocopied love sonnets he was leaving in the funeral home's old milk box and began slipping into Ignatius's bed at night.

But Ignatius couldn't do it with her, not even a wee bit. Ben might have been disappointing in bed, but Skinny Iggy Undertaker was formaldehyde personified. With him a flop, Leelagh took a long look at Gracious who took a long look back and the two of them took to sharing a bed.

Dennis didn't know of any of this. There might have been a hypothesis or two floating about in the faculty lounge at the college, but the lounge wasn't a haunt of his. Gracious had long since graduated and he hadn't seen her around town in ages. He did notice Ben Bobowicz photocopying sonnets in the library but assumed they were for a class.

Ithy, who'd been puzzling over her children lately, puzzled some more and sought comfort from the diner's Greek dishwasher, a bearded fellow who'd bicycled into town one day and claimed to have been an associate professor of mythology at Aristotle University back in Thessaloniki. During his breaks, they'd meet up in the booth back by the waitress station and linger in guarded Greek over baklava and Ithy's bewilderment.

Gracious and Leelagh meanwhile began thinking of the baby-to-be as theirs. Gracious took precautions to keep her pregnancy a secret—consulting with a midwife in another town, not shopping locally once she started to show—until one winter's morning during a snowstorm when, bored, she danced barefoot down the stairs from the flat and on outside without a coat and around the hearse out back in the parking lot. And as she was dancing barefoot in the snow, Mary Meetz from Meetz's Florists happened to pull in with a delivery. The whole town knew by lunchtime. Dennis was dumbfounded.

There are many ways this might have ended. Malicious gossip might have shut down Funk's. Ithy might have fallen in love with the bearded Greek dishwasher, disowned the lot of them, and eloped to the Acropolis. Ben Bobowicz might have tossed a bomb through the funeral home's old milk box and blown the whole place and everyone in it to smithereens. Leelagh Bobowicz, née Laird, might have become a U.S. citizen and run for governor of New Jersey. Gracious might have filed a paternity suit against Dennis to make him feel better.

But here is what actually happened: First, a very healthy if very gaunt baby boy was born to Gracious in a bathtubful of water in the flat on Valentine's Day. She named him Valentine. Ithy tired of the dishwasher's beard, which kept accumulating baklava crumbs and seemed to interfere with his enunciation of alphas, betas, and zetas. She stayed put, fell in love with her grandson, and baby-talked to him in Greek at every opportunity. Also at every opportunity, Leelagh soloed surreptitiously in the embalming room.

Alas, Ignatius began having dizzy spells and dropped dead within a month of being diagnosed with something unmentionable. Gracious put his ashes in one of her urns that hadn't turned out right.

Ben hoped Leelagh would come back to him then and suggested as much but she told him she wanted a divorce and that got him looking for a teaching position as far away as there were any. After committing to memory the spelling of Yoknapatawpha forward and backward and, on the long drive to Mississippi where he had several interviews lined up, listening over and over to the *William Faulkner Audio Collection* on CDs, he was offered a professorship. He eventually remarried, a Southern belle named Estelle, although she never could pronounce Yoknapatawpha, much less spell it.

Ben and Leelagh's house in Saint Plato was put back on the market by Ithy. Gracious and Leelagh remained in the flat with Valentine and left things pretty much untouched downstairs.

Meanwhile, Mr. and Mrs. Edgarty, utterly fed up with Florida, sold their condominium apartment and headed back north, hoping to reestablish themselves in New Jersey. At high noon on the third day of their drive, as they were crossing the Delaware, Mrs. Edgarty suggested they continue on over to Saint Plato and look in on that nice young man, Mr. Funk, and his sweet sister. There they learned of Ignatius's passing and that his funeral home now lacked an undertaker.

And so Mr. Edgarty took up undertaking again, at Funk's, reuniting himself with his hearse and his embalming equipment and whatever other accouterments were lying about, and bought Ben and Leelagh's house for him and Mrs. Edgarty to live in. And Leelagh got to resume her surreptitious embalming. And Valentine got to grow up in a flat above a funeral home with two mothers and his uncle's ashes and become fluent in Greek. And Gracious began cosmetologizing the departed again and making urns again and opened the door when Dennis came to pick up the new urn and flashed him for old time's sake.

# THREE

Would that Denise would swing open her red front door when he pulls up and rush out to him, he would be thrilled. But Dennis does not have a good feeling about what's ahead, the Cruiser at the moment approaching the bridge over the river known as the Bois de Sioux that separates Minnesota and North Dakota. Maybe, just maybe, if he could back up, rewind the last few days, start them over.

But just like that they're across the bridge, he and Sebastian, across the Bois de Sioux and into North Dakota, miles already into North Dakota, turning onto a narrow road that leads to a narrower road that leads to Saint Plato. And just like that they've reached the town, they're on its Main Street, passing its Bijou. *Welcome to Me* is playing, an odd film that Dennis saw in New Jersey, intrigued by Kristen Wiig who was *Me*.

That was then. Now it's straight to Denise's street. Along it.

There's no red front door.

Then there is. It looks like a note is stuck to the door. Dennis's heart thrusts and jabs. He doesn't get out of the car right away. Instead, he tries to calm himself, scratching Sebastian behind his ears, under his chin.

The cat is purring. He rode the whole way lolling about, watching New Jersey go by, Pennsylvania go by. West Virginia, Ohio, Indiana, Illinois, Iowa, Minnesota, a sampling of North Dakota. Their rivers. When inspired he used his litter box, on the floor on the passenger side, balancing in it as the Cruiser cruised along, afterward running short sprints, dashboard to rear window and back, side to side and back.

Dennis tries Denise's number one last time, fantasizing the ringing can reach her. He knows she's not there, hasn't been there for days. He gives up, opens the car's well-weathered white door, gets out, walks up to Denise's red door, the note.

*Life, Dennis! La dolce vita. It's even shorter than I thought.*

*Tuffy and I are off to Alabama, another town called Saint Plato. Can you beat that? It's destino all over again! I've met someone else online. He's curator of a sculpture park of outhouses there. I'm driving mine down in a U-Haul. What a hassle, getting them to rent to me. And they wanted a big deposit. I'd origamied my driver's license, you see, back when I did my library card. I was very into origami at the time. I hope you and Sebastian won't be too disappointed that we're gone. You may linger in the house as long as you like as long as it's not too long. I'm donating the walls to the National Gallery. Arrivederci.*

Dennis is stunned. He knew she wouldn't be there. But still.

The door is unlocked. He brings Sebastian into the house, goes back for the litter box, some cat food, his overnight duffel. It's late afternoon, the sun almost set. The power is on but most of the lights don't work. It seems pleasantly warm inside. Denise's self-portraits are everywhere on the walls. Furnishings are spare. No curtains, no rugs. Books scattered about, splattered with paint. Here and there, candles in empty Chianti bottles. Dribbles of candle wax on the bare wood floors, more splatters of paint.

On the floor in a corner of what might in a normal house be a living room are the phone and the answering machine, unplugged. A tree of some sort, as tall as Dennis and with spreading branches and paint-splattered leaves, dominates the room. Little paper-doll Denises hang from its branches, keeping an eye on the life-size Denises on the walls. The tree is in a large pot and the soil in the pot feels dry. Dennis finds a large bowl next to a pile of empty pizza boxes in the kitchen, fills the bowl with water at the sink, carries it into the living room, pours the water into the pot. An edible slice of leftover pizza in the fridge but he has no appetite for it. Sebastian does, then visits his litter box, then goes scampering up and down the stairs and from room to room.

Like Denise said, her bathroom is odd. Even if the broken toilet were working, one would have to stand or sit at odd angles. Outside, Dennis locates the spot in the backyard where the outhouse most certainly was and pees in the fading light. An old Fiat parked back there.

In Denise's bedroom, her former bedroom, a futon on the floor, blankets, piles of clothes, more candles in more empty Chianti bottles. Dennis lights a few of the candles. As elsewhere, life-size Denises surround him, covering the walls, one self-portrait after another, dressed and partially dressed and more or less undressed. Each Denise looks different from the next. There are Michelle Pfeiffer Denises and Andie MacDowell Denises and Gwyneth Paltrow and Kate Winslett and Scarlett Johansson Denises and on and on. Portraits of Tuffy too, presumably Tuffy, no two alike.

In candlelight, the Denises look older and more sophisticated, younger and more sensual. Mellower, fresher. Happier, sadder. And farther from him than ever.

And svelte. Dennis has always been partial to svelte. Not thin, not slim, not trim, but svelte. Lying on the futon now, taking deep breaths, willing himself to be calm, he embraces svelte. Sebastian has gone to sleep.

*

A ticket on the Cruiser's windshield in the morning, Dennis squinting at it through a beam of sunshine poking into the bedroom. He goes downstairs and on outside to pee, then around front to see about the ticket. It's only a warning—that a town ordinance prohibits toilets from being left overnight on the roof racks of cars.

Sebastian gets Savory Sardines for breakfast and Dennis finds a package of dried figs in a cupboard, paces from room to room as he nibbles, the rooms Denise breathed in, painted in. He tries to count the Denises but they are difficult to count, some partially hidden, some wedged between others at odd angles. He imagines living in the house, he and Sebastian, with the Chianti bottles, the portraits. Surely the National Gallery won't come for the walls.

In the pantry, next to some dried tubes of paint and a jar of stiff paintbrushes, a note: *If you're reading this, you're lingering too long. Arrivederci means arrivederci.*

He takes Sebastian and their stuff out to the Cruiser, asks

someone out jogging for directions to the public library. The jogger points without slowing. Dennis wants to look up Saint Plato, Alabama, and get rid of the toilet, maybe the library would like it, and contemplate the future. An Unhappy Inn would be fitting for tonight.

A librarian sets him up at a computer. Her nametag says *Denise*. She looks like Neve Campbell in *Scream*. Except for her, he's the only person in the library. He's barely typed in *google.com* when *Anything Goes* starts playing. A long moment before he realizes the tune is coming from his cell phone. Molly Minnelli gave him the phone for the trip, his first cell phone ever. Until now it's never rung. He's only used it to call, mostly to call Denise, to try to call her. He doesn't know how to answer it. He pushes one button, another. Nothing happens. The tune starts again. A third button works.

Dennis, *amore mio!* Have you made it to my house yet, you and Sebastian? Do you still love me? Sob. Denise's voice! Her sob.

We stayed there last night, Denise. I watered your tree. I'm at the library now. Sebastian's in the car. I—I haven't stopped loving you.

Then come to Alabama and get me and Tuffy and drive us home! Sob. *Rapidamente!* Sob. *Immediatamente!* Sob. The curator doesn't love me, he just wanted my outhouse. Sob. And I was using it in the U-Haul. I lost my deposit. A string of sobs.

It's okay. I'll come and get you and Tuffy. As immediately as possible.

The sobs stop. Oh, Dennis, *Grazie, grazie, mille grazie!* I just knew you would! We'll be waiting among the outhouses. I'm telling the National Gallery it can't have my walls.

The librarian has come back over. Using a cell phone in the library is not allowed. Dennis isn't listening to her tell him that. He's gotten up. He's so elated, he does what he would never do. He tries to hug her. She screams.

He runs from the building. He never did get to look up anything. Sebastian perks up from a snooze on top of the Cruiser's dashboard, stares at Dennis running to the car, phone pressed to his ear.

36

*Mamma mia!* Denise exclaims. They're still connected.

Who was screaming?

The librarian.

Why?

She didn't want me to hug her.

You were trying to hug the librarian?

I was overcome with joy. By you calling, I mean. Her name's Denise too.

Dennis hurls himself into the car. I'm leaving right now. I'm leaving right now for Alabama. He starts the engine, pulls away. We'll get married as soon as I get there.

Well, no. They can't get married. Not yet. Not legally. There's Mirabelle.

Denise didn't respond anyway, maybe never heard. The call's been dropped.

\*

They're on their way, accompanied by *The Magic Flute.* They stop at that Casey's in Minnesota where Dennis found the Gopher 5 ticket. He asks the clerk to check it, a different clerk— she looks like Michelle Williams in *Shutter Island*—though her nametag also says *Denise.* The lottery screen beeps and bops. The ticket has four of the five numbers from last night's drawing. Dennis has won five hundred dollars.

It's a month to the day since Denise dinged him on Amorous After Fifty. A lucky day, an auspicious day. The clerk counts out his winnings.

The FitzSweeney's Cupcakes van from yesterday is outside. Did you win? the driver asks.

I did! Dennis says.

And you got to keep the toilet!

The toilet? Oh. Uh, yes. Dennis forgot about the toilet. It'll have to ride to Alabama and back. The driver gives him a thumbs-up.

\*

They're back on the highway. Sebastian is playing with a loose strap on the overnight duffel. They'll make it all the way to Iowa today.

And then blue lights are flashing in the rearview mirror. Dennis wasn't speeding, he knows he wasn't speeding. He never speeds. He's never had a speeding ticket in his life. He turns on his blinker, pulls onto the shoulder, pauses *The Magic Flute*. Sebastian stops playing with the strap. An edited version of the past month passes before Dennis's eyes. The past few hours. The librarian. What if she reported him? No, this couldn't be happening.

A skinny trooper comes bounding up to the car. Dennis holds his breath, lowers his window. That toilet on your roof, it's not allowed, the trooper shouts.

Is that why you stopped me? Dennis could hug the trooper. Almost. The toilet's brand new, he says. It's for my fiancée's house in North Dakota.

North Dakota's the other way.

I know. It's a long story.

There's a five hundred dollar fine for transporting toilets on car roofs in Minnesota.

A five hundred dollar fine?

Yeah. New or old. Hey, is that your cat? My sister has a cat.

Oh. What's your sister's cat's name? Humor the man now.

Tuffy.

Tuffy? Uh, what's your sister's name?

Denise.

Denise?

Yeah. Denise Olafsdottir. She's the smartest sister in the world. She skipped grade school.

Olafsdottir, Dennis says softly to himself, then aloud, She's an artist, right?

You've heard of her! Yeah, she paints and stuff. She built an artistic outhouse and took it down to Alabama. It's gonna be on display in a sculpture park. She was pretty excited.

She's not excited anymore. I'm driving down to get her and Tuffy and bring them home. Denise is my fiancée.

You're marrying my sister? Boy, small world, huh? Tell you

what, give me the five hundred now and I'll keep the infraction off your license. It'll be like a wedding gift. Cash if you have it please. Otherwise, make out a check to me: O. Olafsson.

I can give you cash, Dennis says. But O. Olafsson, you say? What does the *O* stand for?

Olaf. It stands for Olaf.

You're Olaf Olafsson? I knew it! You were in the fourth grade in Saint Plato, North Dakota, weren't you? When there was a pen-pal project?

Yeah! Boy, that was a long time ago.

I was in the fourth grade in Saint Plato, New Jersey. I wrote to you. You never wrote back.

I remember that. I did too write back. I wrote, *I'm in the fourth grade too*. But my sister, she was making papier-mâché models of herself and my letter got glued on.

Oh. A long pause. Okay if I go? It's a long way to Alabama.

Sure. As soon as you pay your fine.

You're living in Minnesota now? Dennis asks, handing over the five hundred dollars.

Nah, Olaf Olafsson says, taking the money. I just work both sides of the border. But hot diggity! Lost a lottery ticket somewhere outside a Casey's yesterday. Was playing my sister's phone number. Would've won exactly this much.

*

As Dennis pulls from the shoulder back onto the highway, it starts snowing. Heavy, wet snow. Sebastian watches the wipers push the snow to the edges of the windshield. It's accumulating on the road. Dennis stops at Saint Denise's church again. He'll light a candle, pretend it's a candle in a Chianti bottle that he's lighting. But the church doors are locked today. The Cruiser slips and slides back onto the highway. Past Montevideo, it starts slipping and sliding all over the place. It's not safe to keep driving in the storm. Dennis gets the car to slip and slide up to a motel without a name.

In their room, he and Sebastian look out the window at the wet snow piling up on the car, on the toilet. Dennis wonders if he can find the number in his phone that Denise called from. He can't figure out how. He walks out into the storm and over to a restaurant without a name, orders grilled cheese sandwiches and fish sticks to go, the extent of the menu, brings the food back. The two of them watch the snow fall as they eat.

Molly Minnelli says every snowflake falls exactly where it's meant to, Dennis tells the cat.

Sebastian looks over at him, blinks.

*

*Anything Goes* announces the dawn. Denise! Denise Olafsdottir! Denise Olafsdottir-Dunkle-to-be!

But it's not her. It's Mirabelle's sister. She doesn't have to pull the plug. Mirabelle has become irreversibly dead all on her own. Will he be at the funeral?

No. Just cremate her and send Beverly the ashes for the shoot-out.

Huh?

Just send her the ashes, okay?

Whatever. What's to be done with the house?

Um. You could burn it down and send Beverly those ashes too.

Mirabelle's sister hangs up.

For a moment, for only a moment, Dennis tries to conjure something, anything, that might have been endearing about Mirabelle.

*

The sun has risen bright. The motel parking lot has been cleared. In fact there's no snow anywhere. It's apparently all melted. The air is warm.

Dennis is radiant. Denise is waiting! he tells Sebastian. We can get married in Alabama legally now. We can honeymoon legally all the way back to North Dakota. You and Tuffy can bond in the back seat. From Sebastian, several *irrrphs*.

A few hours along and the Cruiser connects with the

Avenue of the Saints again. The rest of Minnesota whizzes by. Then Iowa. Dennis plays the Bridal Chorus from *Lohengrin* over and over. At stops, he hums *Pachelbel's Canon.*

Years ago, about to say their vows, Mirabelle had demanded something by the Rolling Doors. The Rolling *who?* Dennis and the Justice of the Peace responded together, baffled.

Whaddaya mean *who?* Mirabelle replied, stamping her foot.

They stared at her.

Missouri now. FitzSweeney's Motel. Dennis is told it was named after the owner's parrot.

In the morning the *Avenue of the Saints* signs end at St. Louis and he figures it out. Saint Paul/Saint Louis. He tells Sebastian. The cat scratches his ear.

What if there's a world where an Avenue of the Saints connects all the Saint Platos? Dennis posits to him.

Sebastian rolls over, sighs.

Missouri meanwhile goes on and on. And then Missouri's gone. A slice of Arkansas is next. The wide, wide Mississippi gets crossed again. A corner of Tennessee. And into Mississippi the state.

Alabama is nigh.

Alabama is reached.

Dennis pulls into a truck stop, finds a brochure on the town of Saint Plato, a photograph in the brochure of the sculpture park. A hundred miles to go. It's dark. He'll stop overnight, be there early tomorrow. They'll start back right after the wedding. They'll start back as husband and wife.

Miles and miles along and he can't find a motel. Puccini's *Gianni Schicchi* plays in the dark. Denise might get a kick out of it. Or not. It's very late. Finally, a motel. A sign lit up in front says so: *Finally, a motel.*

*

Dennis turns on the television in the motel room. *International House Hunters* is house-hunting in Italy, a lot of *buongiornos* back and forth. Dennis gives Sebastian a can of

Flounder Feast. When the cat finishes, he washes his face, then scampers into the bathroom, then scampers back out. Dennis imagines he hears the toilet flushing. The cat's asleep on the bed almost before he settles. Dennis lies awake, sleeps briefly, wakes. And so on through the night.

At sunrise, Sebastian is at the window bird-watching, then he's not. The shower is running. Dennis jumps up, rushes into the bathroom. The cat is standing under the spray.

But how—?

Dennis lets him finish, towels him off, quickly showers himself and makes for the dining room, makes a waffle, pours some juice, lingers over the breakfast not at all, fixes a saucer of scrambled eggs, brings it back to the room for Sebastian.

As he's brushing his teeth, he hears a helicopter overhead.

Soon they're in the car, pulling onto the highway. Soon they're in Saint Plato, Alabama, on its Main Street, passing its Bijou. *Rachel Getting Married*. Rosemarie DeWitt fascinated Dennis in it at the Bijou in New Jersey.

He stops to ask directions to the sculpture park and in no time they're approaching the place. His heart is making no sound at all.

Someone is pulling weeds by the gate. Dennis gets out of the car. The weed-puller stands, says, We're not open yet. It says *Curator* on his cap.

I'm here for Denise and Tuffy, Dennis says.

Who? the curator shouts.

Denise and Tuffy, Dennis shouts back.

Oh. Those two. You've missed them.

They're not here?

Left a while ago.

Where'd they go?

Italy.

Italy?

Yeah. They ordered a breakfast pizza and this delivery guy showed up in a red helicopter. He was on his way there with a load of pizza boxes.

But—

Or maybe it was Little Italy. Your friend and her cat got on board before you could say *mozzarella*. You must be Dennis. She said to tell you *scusa*.

Big Italy or Little, Dennis wants to shrivel and die. He can feel himself starting to shrivel and die. Where his mother and Mirabelle failed, Denise might succeed.

But he looks back at the Cruiser, at Sebastian staring through the windshield at him. He has to go on. He can't abandon Sebastian. Sebastian needs him. Sebastian loves him.

Hey, the curator says. I'll take you on a tour. No charge. You can see Denise's outhouse.

She told me you didn't love her, Dennis says. You just wanted the outhouse.

She said that? Saint Plato preserve us!

Dennis forces himself to go on the tour, is shown an extensive collection of outhouses in many inventive shapes and colors. Denise's startles him. It's sort of trapezoidal, sort of something else, and its brilliant shades of red sparkle in the morning sun. He tries to imagine it where it used to be in her backyard in North Dakota and realizes he has to pee.

It wouldn't be right. He walks over to some bushes.

Would you like an indoor toilet? he asks the curator at the end of the tour. It's never been used.

I thought you'd never ask, the curator says. It'll be like exhibiting a Marcel Duchamp.

*

Minus the Duchamp, Dennis leaves the sculpture park, the town. It's a warm day, warm for December, even for the sunny south. Too warm. You might say hot. There's no joy for him in Alabama. He should probably go back. Back to Saint Plato, the New Jersey one.

He pulls off the highway and sits a long time in the Cruiser, his thoughts a muddle. He stares at his cell phone, is tempted to fling it out the window. He'll call Molly Minnelli first. They haven't been in touch since he left for North Dakota, a lifetime ago. Sebastian rubs against him as he tells her of his odyssey, of the ever-present elusiveness of Denise, her namesakes, his heartbreak.

I know some queers who'd take your troubles away, Molly says.

No they wouldn't, Dennis says. How can you joke?

Oh Dennis, dear Dennis, it's only a front. You're not the only one whose heart is broken. Liza Minnelli never answers my letters, you know.

*

They travel on, Dennis and Sebastian, unsure of a final destination. Home was to be North Dakota. With a woman Dennis will never meet. He hadn't meant to ever return to New Jersey. And there's Indianapolis to consider. Of course, he could avoid Indianapolis entirely. But can one really avoid Indianapolis entirely? Didn't Nietzsche address that once?

It starts to rain. Sebastian swishes his tail to the beat of the wipers.

A Very Unhappy Inn overnight. Dennis has dream after dream of loss.

The rain has stopped by morning. On the road, *La Bohème* plays right through to the last act. As Mimi dies, a guinea pig, if that's what it is, skitters into the car's path.

Dennis brakes hard. The Cruiser swerves. The animal skitters from view. Dennis lets up on the brake, straightens the car out, pulls off at a scenic overlook. He ejects the opera, gathers up all the CDs, gets out, marches over to a trash bin, drops them in it. He should dump his stash of Viagra too. Later.

No, now. It's in the miniature sports bag with Sebastian's food. He goes back to the car, collects the pills. Sayonara.

Dennis in the car again. Sebastian rolls onto his back on the passenger seat, looks up at him backwards. *Irrrph*. Dennis rubs him behind his ears.

*

The Cruiser seems headed directly north, headed directly for Indianapolis. Dennis swings east when he can, and swings east again. But Indianapolis remains straight ahead. Through Tennessee and into Kentucky and each swing to the east is met by a twist to the west, maintaining a collision course with Indianapolis. The weather stays quite warm. Hot. Dennis is feeling sticky hot.

The engine starts not sounding right. Sebastian looks at him. Inquisitively. They might not ever get to wherever they're going. They might not ever reach Indianapolis even. They might become stuck in Kentucky.

A hot air balloon way up in the sky now. Dennis slows, watches the balloon, slows more.

A row of little signs along the side of the road:
*In a mile or less*
*You can avoid*
*Indianapoless*
*Turn right soon*
*Follow the balloon*

In a mile or less, Dennis turns right onto a dirt road, eventually comes to a parking area, parks near an old Mustang, the only other vehicle there, *Just Married a Bush Pilot* scrawled across its back window. The Cruiser's engine dies. Sebastian looks all around.

Another sign:
*Hot Air Balloon Rides*
*in Gabriela's Balloon*
*$500*
*Cash Only*

The balloon is descending, is landing, has landed. A most euphoric couple climb from the basket. Dennis recognizes Myrtle Stefanowski from *29 Minutes,* he's sure it's her. Holding hands, laughing, the couple dance over to the Mustang, get in, drive off.

A plump woman climbs from the basket. A very plump woman. It can't be but it must be. Gabriela Gloriosa. Alive and grown wide. Very wide. She's wearing cargo shorts. Her knees are very plump. She bobbles about, checking around the balloon, adjusting stuff.

A dog jumps out of the basket. The dog is very plump.

Sebastian flattens his ears, watches the dog. Dennis scratches Sebastian, tries turning the key in the ignition. The Cruiser's engine starts right up, sounds fine.

The dog starts barking. The cat ducks down. Gabriela Gloriosa looks up, takes a few steps toward the car, calls out, Hello there!

I don't have five hundred dollars in cash, Dennis yells out his window. He backs around, drives quickly away, scratching Sebastian as he drives. They will meet Indianapolis head-on.

*Anything Goes* starts up.

It's Molly.

Hi Dennis. I just hired a new waitress. Guess what her name is.

*

Yes, the new waitress's name is Denise.

But no, she's not North Dakota Denise.

That would be way too bizarre.

# FOUR

Dennis Dunkle's favorite diva fantasy has him in Florida, a librarian in Palm Beach, meeting an operatic Janis Joplin. He's about to indulge in that fantasy now as they're leaving Kentucky, he and Sebastian, crossing into Indiana, being swept north, the Cruiser on some sort of automatic pilot, still aimed directly at Indianapolis.

Whatever will be, Dennis tells Sebastian on the bridge over the Ohio River, Louisville immediately behind them, a plump Gabriela Gloriosa further behind them, and her plump dog and indeed her plump balloon, the river below, the cat impressed with the river, noncommittal about Dennis's nonchalance.

*

He'd been to Palm Beach once in real life, hitchhiking there to see how the half a percent live before shipping out to Vietnam, picked up in Georgia by Harvey and Harriet Hitherto, an agreeable librarian couple from Atlanta on a random holiday. Headed the same way, they drove their jeep right down the Florida coast, right to Palm Beach, stick-shifted around until they spotted a bar, the Taboo on Worth Avenue, parked, and led the way in. Dennis asked for an Our Lady of Saint Plato Pale Ale.

A what? the bartender blurted.

Dennis was carded and ended up back out on the sidewalk looking into shop windows. Harvey and Harriet meanwhile asked for something random on the rocks and, after affably sipping too many rounds, found themselves quite drunk and fancied a midnight drive in the ocean. By then, having looked at length into every shop window on both sides of Worth Avenue, Dennis had climbed into the back of the jeep and gone to sleep. Our jeep, your jeep, Harriet had told him. He woke and leaped out just in time, just as the jeep was about to plow into deep water. Fresh-bruised bones and a gnawed-on gear shift washed up onto the shore in the morning. Rogue groupers, the police speculated.

Not sharks? Dennis asked.

Watch your mouth! they warned. Sharks aren't allowed around Palm Beach.

Dennis likes to believe that his becoming a librarian helped fill a gap Harvey and Harriet Hitherto left in the profession.

*

Janis Joplin had a thing for F. Scott Fitzgerald, and in his fantasy of her Dennis invented parents for himself named Fitzgerald. They were scholars of the author and gave lectures on *The Great Gatsby* all over New Jersey. Their home was a bungalow on an out-of-the-way stretch of Saint Plato Creek and that's where their son, *F. Dennis Fitzgerald,* grew up.

The fantasy's particulars would change and stuff would be added and subtracted over the years, but the way Dennis imagines it today, the Indianapolis skyline looming somewhere beyond the horizon, Janis Joplin is appearing at a rock festival near Palm Beach and he's on his way to it. He's down the stairs from his Worth Avenue apartment over top the Taboo, strutting excitedly past pattering palmetto trees to his car, an old Porsche from Okeechokee Motors out on Okeechokee Trail in West Palm Beach.

He turns the key but the Porsche won't start. It won't start again and again. He tries hitchhiking but hitchhiking is not allowed in Palm Beach. Nor are cars that won't start again and again, even Porsches. The police accost him and he tells them he's the librarian at the town's public library and therefore he has literary immunity. They don't buy that. There's no public library in Palm Beach, they point out.

So far the fantasy is not going well. But fortunately for Dennis, the police are called away to another possible grouper attack.

He never gets to the rock festival though, never gets to see Janis Joplin perform. But he will get even. He will blow up Okeechokee Motors. He will leave no car unturned. He retrieves from a closet in his mind a violin case filled with explosives, left behind in the non-existent library by a blustery fellow in a hurry, most likely intended as a gratuity for the assistance Dennis provided identifying countries without extradition treaties.

Hugging the violin case, he marches righteously across the bridge into West Palm Beach and onward to Okeechokee Trail. As he's closing in on the used car lot, a Mercedes-Benz convertible with its top down pulls up alongside him.

Hey, man, a woman's voice twangs sweetly from the car. Where're you goin' with that violin?

He stops, studies the woman, her wild hair. Jesus! You're Janis Joplin!

The very same, she replies. I'm looking for a good man, preferably one with a violin.

This isn't a violin.

Oh yeah? Janis Joplin jumps from the Mercedes. Lemme see. She grabs at the case. He tries to keep a grip on it, they struggle, it springs open. Sticks of dynamite spill onto the shoulder of the road. Janis Joplin looks puzzled.

Carrots, Dennis explains.

The fudge they're carrots, she says.

Fudge? Did you just say *fudge?* Whoa! You're not Janis Joplin. She would've said *fuck.*

I've sweetened up my act, honey-bun.

You have?

Look. She raises her arms. I've even shaved my armpits.

Hey, cool. And you play the violin?

Well, I sing opera now.

Wow!

So what've you got here, man? It looks like dynamite.

Yeah, Dennis admits. It is dynamite. I'm gonna blow up Okeechokee Motors.

For heaven's sake, no you're not.

They sold me a lemon.

Big fudging deal. C'mon, we'll deep-six these sticks. Janis Joplin collects them, tosses them into the back seat, all but tosses Dennis into the front. They drive past Okeechokee

Motors and on into the boonies. I was just out here somewhere at a rock festival, Janis says. Man, what a bummer! The crowds, the amplifiers, the drugs, everything was freaking me out. I got the words mixed up to Bobby McGee.

That is a bummer, Dennis says.

Yeah, man! Enough of that sugar, I said to myself. It's time to split and find me a Mercedes and a good man.

Where'd you find the Mercedes?

Parked near the courthouse. She pulls over to the edge of the road. I hot-wired it.

This is a stolen car? But you can't just steal a car.

She starts flinging the dynamite into a ditch. I'm gonna hot-wire you next, she says.

Um. You could get into trouble over the car.

You were gonna blow up Okeedokee Motors.

Okee*chokee*, Dennis corrects. And yeah, I was gonna blow the place up. There was a principle involved.

Fiddlesticks.

The dynamite jettisoned, Janis Joplin makes a U-turn and heads back to West Palm Beach, driving all the way downtown to the courthouse and parking the Mercedes where she found it. She jumps out, pulls a wad of money from a pocket of her jeans, and dashes into the building.

Soon she comes dashing back, grinning, cackling, waving a set of keys. All squared, she says. It belonged to the blind dude who sells the chewing gum. Here, take the keys and drive me over to Palm Beach. I left my Zelda Fitzgerald biography at the Breakers. She shoves Dennis behind the wheel.

My name's *F.*, he says. As in F. Scott.

Gerbil-poop.

I'm serious. My full name is F. Dennis Fitzgerald. My parents are F. Scott Fitzgerald scholars. They give lectures on *The Great Gatsby*.

*The Great Gatsby!* Janis Joplin exclaims. Great gosh! I've read that book again and again. Well, half again.

You can call me *Dennis* if you want.

Dennis? Why the fudge would I want to call you *Dennis*? I'll call you F.

He drives to Palm Beach, to the Breakers. You've been staying here? he asks as they approach the stately entrance to the hotel.

On a posh couch in the lobby, she says.

In the lobby, another Janis Joplin is sprawled on just such a couch, reading a book, swigging from a bottle of Southern Comfort.

That's my other self, Dennis's Janis whispers. I split from her. She marches up to her and grabs the book. It's the one she's come for, Zelda's biography.

Hey, bitch! the sprawled Janis shouts. I'm reading that.

Sorry, snookums, Dennis's Janis says. So am I.

The concierge hustles up, emphasizes that shouting is not permitted in the lobby. We're very posh here, he explains, then notices there are two Janises. Egad! Which one of you is you?

It depends, Dennis's Janis says and French-kisses the fellow's ear.

The concierge giggles and says, Oh please do that again.

She does it again. He swoons onto the couch. Janis's other self shoves him off it. Dennis's Janis puts her arms around Dennis, smiles sweetly. Ain't I just like Zelda? she purrs. Crazy and romantic? Ain't I just the craziest, most romantic woman you've ever met? Her eyes gaze into his. Let's go away together, F. Far, far away.

She's so beautiful, so sweet, how can he resist? They skip from the lobby arm in arm. He does glance back though. What about your other self? he asks. She's very upset.

I've washed my hands, his Janis says.

Back in the Mercedes, she French-kisses Dennis's ear. Take me where there are no crowds, no amplifiers, no drugs, she murmurs. The most out-of-the-way place you know.

Um. I guess that would be where I grew up in New Jersey. In a bungalow on Saint Plato Creek. It's *way* out of the way.

Step on it. We'll get married when we get there.

We will?

Violin or not, you're a good man. She does his ear again.

Dennis wonders about leaving his Palm Beach apartment behind, about the library that doesn't exist, his job there.

It's now or never, Janis says.

He chooses *now*.

They've barely hit the road when her magnificent voice starts in on *The Pirates of Penzance*. She sings *a cappella* all the way to Jacksonville.

They stop there, in Jacksonville, and she finds a violin in a pawn shop to accompany herself with. She tunes the strings, rosins up the bow, and back on the highway plunges into *Die Fledermaus*.

That night in Savannah, in an old hotel just off Oglethorpe Square, she takes a long, hot shower, using up all the little bars of soap, enthralling Dennis with *The Mikado*. They've registered as Mr. and Mrs. F. Fitzgerald but Janis insists they remain celibate and wait until they're actually married.

It's December and it gets colder and colder the farther north they drive, unlike the real December, the current one, where it's been much too warm all along Dennis's and Sebastian's route. But Janis won't let Dennis put the top up. It would fudge up my flourishes with the bow, she says and resumes *L'Elisir d'Amore* with an unfudged-up flourish. As they check into a funky motor lodge near Richmond, Dennis is shivering non-stop. Janis teases that they should go for a swim in the leaf-strewn outdoor pool.

*

*Die Meistersinger* explodes from her the next morning as they're crossing a scary bridge arching high above the Potomac. Oh, man, this is like *La Scala* on wheels! she exults. She grins the biggest grin Dennis would ever see—except he's afraid to look over at her and risk catching a frightening glimpse of how high up they are.

Look, Mr. Ed Sullivan, wherever you are, no hands! she yells later in the day, holding hers high, after belting out something from *Fidelio*. It's suppertime and they're in Delaware, stuck in rush-hour traffic in downtown Wilmington as they look for a restaurant. I should've sung *that* on his show, she tells Dennis.

Jesus, Janis! he says, People are staring and I'm fucking

freezing.

I'm gonna wash your mouth out with soap, she threatens.

In a motel cabin that night in New Jersey, she hums Vivaldi's *Winter* on and off in her sleep.

On the road in the morning, it's *The Marriage of Figaro*. By the time they reach Saint Plato, Janis is hoarse. They stop for throat drops at the A to Y Apothecary.

Soon they're at the creek, driving up to the bungalow. It's closed up. Dennis's parents are now giving lectures on *The Great Gatsby* all over Arizona. Janis jimmies the lock, charges inside, kicks the color TV, and smacks the phone. Everything starts working. She makes a few calls and tracks down a minister to marry them.

Just as snowflakes begin to fall and the fireflies come out, the minister arrives. It's the wrong season for fireflies, but they and the snowflakes look magnificent together as Dennis and Janis say their vows.

*

Their first winter at the bungalow is idyllic. They mostly keep to themselves and have great sex and watch *Dialing for Dollars* a lot. Janis sings arias while making pancakes for breakfast. Sometimes they go outside and make angels in the snow, her magnificent heaps of hair sparkling with ice crystals in the winter sun. Now and then they drive into Saint Plato and paint it pastel. Janis acquires an old upright piano and hammers out stirring preludes and finales. She practices yoga on the piano bench. She puts Modigliani prints on the walls and adopts a large fluffy white cat named Sebastian from the animal shelter.

In the spring they put up a white picket fence. They start visiting a nearby wildlife refuge. Janis loves the peacefulness of the refuge. She sings *bel canto* to the wildlife.

Come summer they skinny-dip in the creek on hot afternoons. One hot afternoon, a fellow named Herman—as in Melville, he stresses—moves into a bungalow down the lane with Patsy Cline. They have a canoe. The four of them become friends and go canoeing in the creek on weekends. As Dennis and Herman paddle, Janis and Patsy improvise duets from *Così Fan Tutte.*

Aren't we like dead? Patsy asks Janis once.

Not exactly, Janis replies.

Dennis's application for a position at the Saint Plato Public Library is discarded. He's never interviewed. Under Professional Experience he listed the non-existent library in Palm Beach and was disqualified for falsifying his employment history. But income's not an issue. Janis has unlimited wads of money in the pockets of her jeans.

*

One night in the fall she wakes in a sweat and frantically shakes Dennis awake.

F.? My other self? I just had a dream she's gonna OD.

They call around, unsuccessfully. Snookums is in terrible trouble and I don't know where she is, Janis laments. It isn't until much later that she remembers an old hotel she used to stay at in Los Angeles, and that's where they find her, where she's found, in her room there, too late.

You dumb cluck! Janis screams at herself across three thousand miles and the life/death divide.

Wearing a disguise, she flies to California, joins mourners in farewells to herself, watches her ashes being scattered, flies back. Dennis meets her at the Newark airport and, after a long embrace, she looks up at him and says, let's make a baby, okay? Soon she is pregnant with Zeldique.

She has more dreams about the future and based on them begins telling fortunes *pro bono,* helping others avoid misfortunes. Sometimes a dream is too vague to be of much use—or too late, like the one about her other self—but most of them are to the point and timely. Word gets around about the fortune-telling and she helps many people.

Their own family has its growing pains. On one occasion, François, their youngest, crayons the piano keys and eats the crayons. Another time, Zeldique breaks the strings on her tennis racket and replaces them with the strings from her mother's violin.

The kids grow up, leave home, get married themselves. There's a new color TV, a new Mercedes, grandchildren, a grand piano, a grand Stradivarius, more large fluffy white cats. Janis names them all Sebastian.

She reads with interest the biographies of her other self as they're published. When the musical *Love, Janis* opens in New York, she and Dennis attend, Janis forsaking opera for the night and humming along to the songs. She's wearing a disguise again and no one takes any notice.

Hey, what if I understudy myself, she whispers to Dennis, and throw in a ditty from *Aida?*

\*

One day a happy-go-lucky dental hygienist from Hoboken knocks on their bungalow door wanting to have her fortune told. Heavens to Betsy! Janis exclaims when she opens the door, recognizing her from a dream. Something bad happens to you in an undisclosed location. Don't go there.

The dental hygienist is miffed. Why on earth would I go to an undisclosed location?

Doggone if I know, Janis says. Undisclosed locations have been in the news lately.

Get real. I'm just a happy-go-lucky dental hygienist from Hoboken. And, by the way, my name isn't Betsy.

\*

Down the road a month, Janis and Dennis are breezing along with the top down, on their way home from the farmers' market, when a masked man on a silver Fatboy cuts them off.

Nit-brain! Janis yells and throws a tomato at him.

They jump from the Mercedes and the masked man hops off the motorcycle. It falls over. Mrs. Fitzgerald? he calls, striding toward her, brushing tomato bits from his shirt. You're in a big pickle. That happy-go-lucky dental hygienist from

Hoboken? We nabbed her at her work. The place was crawling with terrorists waiting to have their teeth cleaned. We took her to an undisclosed location and threatened her with root canals until she spilled the beans. He pokes a finger at Janis and shouts, You were in cahoots with her.

I was not! Janis shrieks, poking back. I don't even know her name. Except it's not Betsy. It's just that I'd had a psychic dream and she was in it and—

You had a psychic dream? Ha. That's rich. And I'm Tonto.

No, you're not. You're not the Lone Ranger either. You're a nit-brain with tomato on your shirt. I've been having psychic dreams for years. Once I dreamt my original self was gonna OD. There were two of me. I'm the former Janis Joplin.

The former who? The former Benedict Arnold would be more like it.

Oh, go fudge yourself! Janis shrieks, lunging at him. Just go fudge yourself. She knocks him to the ground and sits on him.

Janis! Dennis says. Be careful!

She shrieks on. I'm just as patriotic as what's his name— you know, F. Scott Key. She wails *The Star-Spangled Banner* from start to finish.

A tear trickles from underneath the masked man's mask. Okay, so maybe you weren't in cahoots, he concedes when Janis is done wailing and lets him up.

So are you gonna arrest me for the tomato or anything? she asks.

Aw, let's forget it, he says. Besides, if you're Janis Joplin, you're dead. I can't arrest a dead person. He goes and rights the Fatboy, starts it up, yells, Hi, ho, Fatboy! and roars off. Janis mumbles to herself.

\*

Dennis pauses the fantasy here to reminisce about listening to *The Lone Ranger* on the radio when he was a kid. And *Captain Midnight*. And *Sky King*, making believe he was Penny's boyfriend. And he remembers those times in grade school coming home for lunch, his mother ignoring him, locking herself in the pantry to listen to *The Romance of Helen Trent*. Stupid woman! his mother grumbled one day coming out of the pantry.

He hurries back to make-believe just in time for the nation's first transsexual President to be elected. An environmentalist, the President moves the White House to New Jersey, to the nearby wildlife refuge, leaving a big hole in the ground in Washington, D.C.

*

Early one hot midsummer morning Janis frantically shakes Dennis awake, like that other time.

F.? I've just had a whopper of an ominous dream. Little orange men with comb-overs and evil smirks are crash-landing a malevolent-looking spaceship in the Rose Garden as I speak. They're gonna try to take over the world. They've gotta be stopped. I gotta warn the President. She pulls the phone onto the bed. Dennis looks up the local number for the Oval Office.

Janis dials. The President answers. The world is in grave danger, Janis says, and tells why.

Goosefeathers! the President whines when she's finished. I'm worn out, my back aches. I just pruned all the rose bushes and came inside and showered. Now I gotta go back out there and deal with *this?*

You'd better or it'll be the end of the world as we know it, Janis says.

*

That afternoon a rejuvenated, giddy President bicycles up to the bungalow, hugs Janis and Dennis, hands them a pile of roses from the bicycle basket, and half out of breath says excitedly, The world is saved! A malevolent-looking spaceship *had* crash-landed in the Rose Garden, right on top of an American Beauty bush! Little orange men with comb-overs and evil smirks were hobbling all around! An incapacitated

57

phalanx of sniveling blunderbusses, my speechwriter would have me say. I rounded up every last one of them and put them in Mason jars!

They settle in the living room and celebrate with a six-pack of Our Lady of Saint Plato Pale Ale. Janis has kept taking in large fluffy white cats and the room is overrun with Sebastians going *irrrph*.

The President tells her she'll get a hero's medal.

Oh, wow! Can it say *Janis Joplin* on it? she asks. I'm the former Janis Joplin.

The President stares very hard at her. *The* Janis Joplin?

You bet your bleeping buttocks.

I used to be a big fan of yours. But you're dead. No one will buy this.

There were two of me, she says, jumping up. I'm the one who sings opera now.

You mean like *To-re-a-dor-o?*

Something like that. She walks over to the President. Work something out, buttercup. I want to be in an HBO documentary. And sing patriotic arias during seventh-inning stretches. She French-kisses both of the President's ears.

The President blushes, recovers, says, This is absurd.

Cats are climbing all over.

My wife helped save the world, Dennis puts in.

Yes, the President concurs. And the world is in her debt. But it would be best if we keep it to ourselves. We need to forget about HBO and seventh-inning stretches.

Well, fudge, Janis says.

Tell you what, the President says after a pause. If it would make you feel better, I could get you into an alternate ending of an episode of *Buffy the Vampire Slayer.*

You could do that? she asks.

Piece of cake. You wouldn't believe the powers of this office.

*

At the White House, after an intimate hero's banquet, the President links arms with Janis and Dennis and they go and inspect the Mason jars. All the little orange men smirk. For crying out loud! Janis says and sticks her tongue out at them.

The inspection completed, the three of them gather around a television in the East Wing and watch an episode of *Buffy the Vampire Slayer*. In it, Janis obliterates a cemeteryful of vampires. When it's over, a secret service agent is commandeered as a fourth for bridge. Janis bids and makes a grand slam.

They've been drinking and Janis especially is tipsy now and she keeps eyeing the President with curiosity. Hey, let's play strip poker, she finally says.

They're down to their underwear when Dennis stops to pee at a Circle K. The Indianapolis skyline is behind in the distance. The Cruiser is pointed east. He's fantasized right through Indianapolis. He was so into the fantasy that he has no recollection of the drive.

I'm on my way home, he announces gleefully to the Circle K clerk as he's leaving the store.

That's nice, she responds faintly, eyeing him oddly. She has no nametag and doesn't look like anybody.

His glee is undampened. New Jersey here we come! he beams as he gets back into the car.

Sebastian's been napping on the passenger seat. He stirs, opens one eye, closes it, and nudges himself back into a white fluffy ball.

# PART II
# ELSEWHERE

# FIVE

Elsewhere—in another world actually—Dennis Dunkle is in his office trying to make sense of Haruki Murakami's latest novel, a recent library acquisition. But he can't focus. He's been feeling anxious of late, not getting enough sleep, and at the moment he's feeling guilty for telling Molly Minnelli to go fuck a duck. That was last night as she was going on and on about him joining Amorous After Fifty. I don't fuck ducks! she'd shouted back at him. Maybe he should phone her now, apologize, give in, agree to join.

Maybe not. Skateboard wheels are rolling tither and hither over in Periodicals. He comes out of his office to investigate. Ah! It's Freddy Gonzalez-Schmidt skateboarding about, Saint Plato's peculiar doctor, presumably in quest of some peculiar medical fact. What better time to mention the anxiety, the insomnia, the guilt?

*Nicht zu vorry*, Freddy says, apprised, reaching into his fanny pack as he wiggles to stay balanced on his board. He pulls out a prescription pad, scribbles on the top slip, tears it off, and hands it to Dennis with a *Buenos días, amigo*.

*Gracias*, Dennis responds.

Geronimo! Freddy shouts, skateboarding wildly into the next aisle.

Dennis takes the slip to the A to Y Apothecary.

Where he meets Julia.

In this particular world, Julia is the new pharmacist at the A to Y Apothecary.

Julia is svelte. Julia is stunning. She smiles when Dennis gives her Freddy's prescription slip. She looks like Julia Roberts in *Mona Lisa Smile*.

And she's way too young. Nevertheless, pills in hand, Dennis invites her to Mozart's *Don Giovanni*. The college's performing arts department is staging it in Fedankgo Auditorium at the weekend.

Gee, I can't, Julia says, moving her soft lips sensually. I'll be in the Kittatinny Mountains at an enlightenment intensive.

An enlightenment intensive? I've always wanted to do something like that, he says. I could skip the opera. Are there still openings, do you think?

Probably, she says slowly. But there's no socializing, it's a rule.

But there'll be opportunities, Dennis is sure of that. He returns to the college, registers online, sees that participants can bring their cats.

We're getting enlightened this weekend, he tells Sebastian when he gets home.

*Irrrph.*

Sebastian and I are getting enlightened this weekend, he tells Molly later, walking into the diner. She glares at him. He mentions Julia. She glares some more. Look, I'm sorry for telling you to go fuck a duck, he says.

Julia? Molly smirks, ignoring Dennis's apology. Is that her name? I've seen her in here. She looks barely old enough not to be a minor. Are you trying to out-lech Silas?

Meaning Silas Punterponk, taking in their exchange from several stools down, a mug of Supremo in front of him, the diner's famous coffee brewed from New Jersey beans. I've already made my move, he confides. Tried to. She's a ninny. *Dennis* might consider a duck.

Molly bursts out laughing.

Dennis slinks out, embarrassed. Yet adamant. He returns to the A to Y Apothecary the next morning, tells Julia he's registered, invites her to lunch. Gee, I can't, she says. I'm meditating for lunch.

Oh.

He stays to buy a travel tube of toothpaste. Didn't you read the rules? Julia says. You're not supposed to bring your own toothpaste. It'll be supplied.

But he might not like the brand that will be supplied. He's bringing his own deodorant as well, which is also on the list of things not to bring. Unlike toothpaste, however, it's not going to be supplied. And he won't be smelly around Julia, no way.

*

So now he's tooling toward the Kittatinny Enlightenment Center, fantasizing that he and Sebastian and Julia will become enlightened together, fantasizing Julia will be inside the Quick Chek just ahead buying deodorant. She's not. Farther along, he stops at a scenic overlook, walks around, and spots a woman who looks like his comatose wife, Mirabelle. He rushes back to the car.

Reaching the center, people hugging each other out in front, Dennis fantasizes Julia will hug him, Sebastian too, when they first cross paths. At the reception desk, he sees her sitting on a bench over to the side in animated conversation with some other guy. He walks over. Julia looks up at him blankly, looks at Sebastian with alarm, composes herself, and introduces Cedric, who's also a participant, a weightlifter from Weehawken. Without the stops, Dennis might've been there first. He, not Cedric, might be sitting on the bench in animated conversation with Julia.

There's no hug from her. She doesn't get up. But Cedric, quite muscular and ruddy, does. He hugs Dennis vigorously, then picks up Sebastian and tries to hug him vigorously too. The cat hisses at him.

A coughing, wheezing woman soon appears, not svelte, not stunning, not young, the woman running the intensive. She looks like someone in some movie Dennis walked out of. Her name is Faith. She gathers everyone in the enlightenment room. They recline on the floor on backjack chairs. Sebastian sits on Dennis's lap.

You're here to wake up to who you really are, Faith wheezes. To get rid of all the garbage that's plastered over your true selves. But you're not going to do it like the Buddha did. It took that old fart forever. The technique you will use will have you enlightened before you leave. Guaranteed.

Yeah, sure, Dennis thinks. He sees Julia writing in a notebook—whatever for?— looking too serious, unappealing.

Faith blows her nose, explains the exercises—breaking

off into pairs, instructing each other over and over to *Tell me who you are,* changing partners every half hour. They've been getting enlightened like this in California for years, she says.

Julia keeps taking notes.

Cedric asks if there will be an agreement of confidentiality for the weekend.

No, Faith coughs.

Why not? someone else asks, a woman Dennis hadn't noticed, a tabby cat on her lap. She looks like Meg Ryan in *Kate and Leopold.*

Because I say so, Faith wheezes.

*

She's an artist, a painter, Dennis learns after they bump into each other in the middle of the night, one coming out of, one going into a bathroom. She lives somewhere in the Kittatinny Mountains, too complicated to explain just where. Her name is Denise.

I can't sleep, she whispers.

Neither can I, Dennis whispers back. My cat's fast asleep though.

Mine too, she says.

They go out on the porch, sit in rocking chairs, rock. Denise tells him she's studied philosophy too. Her cat's name is Tuffy.

Dennis tells her about Julia, that he came to the intensive because of her, how absurd that was, but now he's glad he's here, glad he's met Denise, he hopes that doesn't make him seem, well, you know. Denise smiles, says absurdity has its pluses, says she's glad he's here too, she's glad she's met him, maybe she'll paint his portrait on her bedroom wall someday. Maybe someday soon. A thrill flows through him. They squeeze hands and rock a while longer before returning to their dormitory rooms.

Dennis cuddles next to Sebastian, closes his eyes, and drifts off, right into the path of an annoying pinging sound followed by a wheezing voice. This is the first full day of your enlightenment intensive, the voice wheezes. Rise and fucking shine. Sebastian stays curled up asleep on the bed.

Minutes later, his face washed, his teeth brushed with his own toothpaste, his deodorant applied, Dennis props himself in a backjack chair next to Denise. Faith coughs up a few more words and the backjacks are moved around and Dennis and Denise are facing each other. Tell me who you are, she says to him, mimicking a Transylvanian accent.

Dennis looks into her eyes, responds, I'm a vampire who thirsts for you.

Denise smiles. She reaches across to him, touches his hand.

No touching! Faith coughs. And talk loud! Yell!

We'll distract each other, Julia objects. She's sitting opposite Cedric. Everyone had begun in a low voice.

Not if you're focused, Faith wheezes. You should be screaming that you hate your fucking lives.

The participants gawk at her. She snorts, You've got to let go so you can say *fuck this* and *fuck that* and not care what anyone thinks and by tonight all of you could be enlightened.

Denise looks at Dennis and whispers, Fuck her.

Dennis tries to muffle a laugh.

No laughing! Faith barks, getting up. She walks over to them. You're not ready to laugh. Now give her her instruction.

You mean, *Tell me who you are?*

No! I mean her instruction on how to build a Buddha with Legos.

Dennis takes a deep breath, ignoring Faith's sarcasm or whatever it was, and asks Denise to tell him who she is. Denise closes her eyes and pretends to meditate. Faith remains, hanging over them. Denise keeps her eyes closed. And keeps her eyes closed. And keeps her eyes closed.

Look, Faith wheezes. Your life is a mess. That's why you're here, isn't it? To clean up the mess and become enlightened? Aren't you angry about your life? Wouldn't you like to scream and pound the floor?

Denise opens her eyes, stares up at Faith. Why would I want to scream and pound the floor? she says. I like my life.

I like her life too, Dennis says.

Vishnu almighty, Faith mumbles. She leaves them, goes

down the row, and hovers over Cedric who's just announced to Julia that he's a big pink flamingo.

Denise looks at Dennis and whispers, I'm a sexy redhead who wants to bite your lip.

They break for tea and there's another exercise and then breakfast. Sebastian and Tuffy join them for breakfast, devouring the vegetarian bacon, licking the butter and maple syrup off the whole grain waffles.

Then more exercises. Julia avoids Dennis and doesn't seem to notice that he doesn't seem to notice. Later, outside during what Faith calls *walking meditation,* Denise and Dennis sneak off and nestle in each other's arms in the woods. She bites his lip.

Several participants get lost walking and, to make up for them back in the enlightenment room, Faith integrates the cats into the exercises. Sebastian responds to each *Tell me who you are* with an *irrrph* and likewise gives the instruction with one. Tuffy rolls onto her back and purrs no matter what. Faith pronounces both cats enlightened. When it's Dennis's turn to sit opposite Sebastian, he jumps up after an *irrrph* and shouts that he's the Incredible Hulk.

From several backjacks over, Julia looks at him with alarm, calls out, I must've given you the wrong pills.

Incredible, Faith snorts.

Halfway through lunch, a woman tosses down her soup spoon and stomps from the table. At the door she turns around and screeches, Stupid waste of my weekend.

Dennis freezes. She looks like the woman at the scenic overlook who looked like Mirabelle.

That's the first passion you've shown here, Faith calls to her.

You want passion? The woman stomps back to the table, picks up her bowl of soup, carries it over to Faith, and dumps the soup on her head.

I won't take this personally, Faith responds, noodles sliding down her face.

The woman stomps out the door with a *Whatever* and is gone.

Dennis is relieved. Denise giggles. Julia looks distressed. The others continue eating quietly.

That afternoon Cedric suddenly shouts, Yes! I'm *that!* He jumps up and waves his arms over his head. *That!* He runs outside and over to a tree and climbs up into it.

He's *what?* Julia asks.

Lordy, Faith coughs.

When Dennis and Julia pair off and he instructs her to tell him who she is, she excuses herself and goes and locks herself in a bathroom.

\*

After lights out, approaching midnight, Dennis and Denise meet in the laundry room and make love in a pile of crumpled sheets, violating the intensive's Rule No. 9 — *No sex of any kind.*

We were so quiet, Dennis whispers afterward. Maybe it wasn't sex.

Oh, it was sex all right, Denise giggles.

Sebastian and Tuffy find them and burrow into the sheets themselves.

Denise giggles some more. Maybe we could do it again, out loud, and wake everyone up, she teases. You know, enlighten them!

They do it again, slowly, quietly, then cuddle in each other's arms in the crumpled sheets.

\*

That annoying pinging sound. This is your last day to get enlightened, Faith wheezes at the door to the laundry room. Did you have a good fuck?

Yes, thank you, Denise responds evenly. Several.

Before the first exercise, Faith instructs Dennis to tell everyone what, if anything, he realized overnight during his sleeping meditation.

Dennis stares at Faith, looks over at Denise, closes his eyes, opens them, looks at Denise some more. Um, he says, I'm not sure. I didn't sleep much. Denise and I spent the night making love in the laundry room.

That's against the rules! Julia shouts.

Keep quiet! Faith coughs, then to Dennis, Tell us what you realized during your sex meditation.

Some of the others giggle. Denise moves over next to Dennis, takes his hand. She looks radiant. Sebastian and Tuffy amble in, flop down in front of them.

Dennis kisses Denise. I guess I realized that there's nothing to realize, he says.

Denise snuggles against him, says, Yes! That's it! There's nothing to realize.

Faith looks at them with reverence, coughs, and says, As have your cats, you two surely have attained total fucking enlightenment.

It doesn't count! Julia shouts. They broke the rules! It doesn't count!

Oh, shut up! Faith shouts back, then starts muttering to herself. She has the group break for tea.

As Julia gets up, Cedric comes over and whispers into her ear. She seems puzzled, then abruptly brushes past everyone, marches outside, and goes swinging from limb to limb in Cedric's tree. Eventually she drops down from the tree, marches back in, grabs Cedric's cup from his hands, drinks the rest of his tea in several big gulps, sets the cup aside, slides her hands up underneath his shirt, lifts her soft, sensual lips toward his, and murmurs, Enlighten my brains out, you Weehawken weightlifter, you!

The intensive ends after lunch. Faith advises the participants to wait before making major changes in their lives. Unless they can't wait. Some of them can't.

Julia phones the A to Y Apothecary to say she won't be back that day or the day after that or the day after the day after that or ever. She gets in her car and follows Cedric to Weehawken.

Dennis also makes a phone call, to the college library. He also won't return to Saint Plato. He and Sebastian will follow Denise and Tuffy to wherever it is in the Kittatinny Mountains that they live, wherever it is that was too complicated for Denise to explain.

But his car won't start. Dennis and Sebastian sit in it watching Denise's fade from view, Tuffy looking out the rear window at them.

# SIX

Indeed there is a world where an Avenue of the Saints connects all the Saint Platos, exactly as the original Dennis Dunkle once posited to his cat. You can drive from Bijou to Bijou to Bijou just by following the *Saints* signs. But the Dennis Dunkle in that world never does. He never joins Amorous After Fifty. He never becomes a librarian either. He suffers innumerable blows to the head and becomes an anthropologist instead.

Among the early blows: When he refuses to eat the poisoned hot dog his mother has prepared for him, she lifts him up, flips him over, and drops him on his head. Returning home from his mission to FitzSweeney Wash and Fold, his bike hits a pothole, he's thrown, and his head collides with Atlantic Avenue. When he won't tell his mother where he got a fortune cookie the Chinese FitzSweeneys gave him, she grabs the cookie and eats it herself, the fortune still inside it, unread, then bashes his skull with a frying pan. During a fourth grade recess out on the school playground, Gabriela Gloriosa haphazardly flings a baseball into the air and on its way down it beans him.

He isn't into pretend baseball cards or pretend catalog cards. Rather, he becomes obsessed with a band of Native American Indians who roamed that world's New Jersey before emigrating during New Jersey's potato famine. He turns his bedroom into his own private Saint Plato Emigrant Museum, covering the walls with drawings he makes of the famished Indians paddling their canoes out to the mouth of Saint Plato Creek and out into the Gulf Stream and thence to Ireland.

With his Emigrant Museum established, instead of the usual firecracker to wake Dennis on his next birthday, his mother hurls a tomahawk at him. It slices into his pillow inches from his head. Damn! she shouts. Wide right! Why don't *you* go scalp yourself and save me the trouble!

His head's not out of the woods. In Vietnam, when that

72

sergeant from Bemidji walks off toward the toilet and it's destroyed by a friendly mortar, the portable record player conveying the smoldering *Pagliacci* is flung into the air by the concussion from the explosion and crashes down guess where.

Back home, the GI bill gets Dennis to anthropology school where Mirabelle isn't and he thereby avoids meeting and marrying her. He obtains a master's degree in anthropology and begins pursuit of a PhD, envisioning research in Ireland among descendants of the New Jersey Indians. But his GI benefits run out and the school rejects his application for a fellowship. It's only granting fellowships to students envisioning research among exotic peoples. The New Jersey Indians aren't on its exotic list.

Short of funds, Dennis drops out of the PhD program. But all is not lost. Molly Minnelli stakes him to a couple of months rent on a small storefront next to Lulu's Laundromat on Main Street. There isn't room inside for much more than a desk, a few chairs, some bookshelves, a cot to sleep on, and Lulu's loud, piercing laugh that now and then intrudes from the Laundromat. Molly helps Dennis organize the space and they put up his old drawings from his childhood Emigrant Museum and posters of Margaret Mead in New Guinea and Claude Lévi-Strauss in who knows where and hang out a sign that says *Anthropologist*.

A few people are tempted to come in if only to snoop, but they steer clear, perhaps not wanting to be seen by anyone who knows them. Most likely they instruct their daughters to cross to the other side of the street when passing the place.

Dennis's mother doesn't cross to the other side of the street. She barges right in with a poisoned asparagus sandwich for his lunch. It only smells as funny as asparagus usually smells, but he dumps it into the trash anyway. It's actually not poisoned. His mother mistakenly made the sandwich with the unpoisoned spears she was saving for herself. She eyes the posters, scoffs that Margaret Mead and what's-his-face look perverse, barges back out, goes home, and eats the spears meant for Dennis.

Shortly after her cremation, a large fluffy white cat ambles into the storefront and makes himself at home. He's wearing a nametag that says *Sebastian*. Lulu tells Dennis he ambled off a Greyhound bus. Her Laundromat is the Greyhound stop in town.

A woman with a fistful of money is next. She directs a *humpf* at Dennis's emigrant drawings, then counts out five hundred dollars and asks if it'll be enough for a kinship chart. Sebastian sniffs the money. Dennis says it's probably too much. The woman says it would be a complicated chart, Exhibit No. 1 in a legal matter.

Oh-oh. Dennis skipped the complicated-kinship-chart seminar in anthropology school. He keeps quiet about that. The woman talks on, introduces herself as Gogaleen Gogginy, a former Fewest-Freckle Queen in FitzSweeney, Ireland.

FitzSweeney? Dennis asks. There's a town in Ireland called FitzSweeney?

I had a pub there, Gogaleen Gogginy says. I lost it playing flinch with a cannibal on holiday. He and his family were planning to stay on.

Hmmm. Are there a lot of FitzSweeneys in FitzSweeney?

None, she says. They were all massacred by the New Jersey Indians.

By the New Jersey Indians?

No more of them either.

No more Indians?

One too many potato famines. My ex-lover-creep is the last surviving descendant. He took me here after I lost the pub, got me pregnant on the way over. What a drag, morning sickness in a canoe.

In a canoe? You came here in a canoe?

He's afraid of flying. But, hey, I hit the jackpot in Atlantic City and bought a grand house on East Avenue. I'd enough jackpot left over to buy all of East Avenue but I was still entitled to child support from my ex's uncle's stepdaughter's cousin's boyfriend.

Huh?

It's a tradition among the New Jersey Indians. The father's not responsible. His uncle's stepdaughter's cousin's boyfriend is.

But if your ex is the last surviving descendant, there

wouldn't be an uncle or anyone.

Some things in a parallel world are inexplicable.

What's a parallel world?

This one. If you'd become a librarian, you'd know stuff like that. So what happened is the cousin's boyfriend was paying support but then he lost her to my ex shooting hoops and my ex left me and became *her* boyfriend. Good riddance! He never fit in on East Avenue, especially after he put up that basketball rigamagig in the driveway. You'd think *he'd* be paying me support now. But no, the creep claims that being her boyfriend doesn't matter if he's also the father, they cancel each other out or something.

Little of what Gogaleen Gogginy has been saying makes sense to Dennis. Actually none of what she's been saying makes sense to him. But he signs on. At the very least, he'll be able to discuss anthropological stuff with the Indian during recesses.

He begins preparing for the trial by reading meticulously through kinship chart primers from the college library and poring over studies of kinship traditions, although he finds none like the father's-uncle's-stepdaughter's-cousin's-boyfriend one. Missionaries' accounts of the New Jersey Indians yield only complaints about sunburn and frostbite and salt air and savagery. Nevertheless, bit by complicated bit Dennis is able to construct a chart, putting in names Gogaleen Gogginy provides, surmising where there are gaps. He makes a large drawing of the chart to display in the courtroom and practices testifying in front of a mirror.

It takes a whole week for all the testimony to be heard and there are plenty of recesses for Dennis to discuss anthropological stuff with the Indian. But the Indian refuses to discuss anything with him. You're on the side of former fewest-freckle face, he says. She can't paddle canoe worth shit.

When Dennis is on the stand—he's called back several times to explain portions of the chart—Sebastian sits on his lap. Attorneys on both sides come up and pet the cat. The court reporter keeps a tally. Her nametag says *Denise*. She looks like Emily Blunt in *Salmon Fishing in the Yemen*. Midweek she slips

Dennis a slip of paper with her phone number on it. But when he dials it that night, stomach aflutter, a recording tells him there's no such number.

There's no jury either. After closing arguments and Denise's report that the two sides petted Sebastian an equal number of times, the judge announces he's deadlocked. Court is adjourned for the weekend.

*

Here's one for the law books, the judge announces Monday from the bench, the kinship chart beside him. Before heading home Friday, I had a few snorts with Denise, er, the court reporter, um, *ex* court reporter. She's had to resign, workplace policy, you know, potential conflicts of interests and all that brouhaha. But better her than me. Wow, is she hot! I consulted my horoscope about our future and it said, Are you in for a surprise! So I phoned one of those hotline psychics and was told it would be the mother of all surprises. And today before anyone showed up here in court I was idly staring at the kinship chart, and you could've knocked me over *without* a feather, look, Denise is in it, way over in this corner, where I'm pointing, she's also a cousin of the uncle's stepdaughter, and *I'm* her boyfriend. Oh boy! Forget about that other cousin and the screwy canoer. *I'm* responsible for the Gogginy kid!

It's the lead story in the *Weekly Banner*.

He himself could have been the boyfriend, Dennis realizes, had Denise's number not been not a number. There's little time to dwell on the implications of that, however. Practically overnight, publicity from the case becomes a boon for his anthropology business. First off, the New Jersey branch of Archaeologists Anonymous commissions him to oversee a dig under the J.C. Penney store on Main Street. An adolescent Gracious Funk dances past the dig on and off and flashes him. But surely not, he must be seeing things.

Fedankgo's Family Restaurant has him reconstruct an extinct society's recipe for an exotic dish of raw and cooked parts. Most of the customers ordering the dish use a lot of ketchup on it and some of them throw up, including the Gogginy judge. They're mollified after further research by Dennis indicates it was the goal of the extinct eaters to throw up. And shame on those who didn't. Well, shame on me! the judge's girlfriend, ex-court reporter Denise, is overheard crowing.

A glee club engages Dennis to track down traditional incantations once incanted by Polynesian outrigger paddlers from the now defunct South Pacific Theme Park outside town. At Fedankgo's Saloon he records inebriated patrons incanting incantations they remember from when the paddlers used to drunkenly incant there.

Teenagers pile into the office wanting to run away and come of age in Samoa. For a small fee Dennis talks them out of it.

And so on and so forth until Joyce Carol Oates shows up. Not the famous author Joyce Carol Oates in that world but the Joyce Carol Oates who's a hairdresser in town, the only daughter of Dick and Judy Oates of South Saint Plato, rhubarb farmers now deceased. Ms. Oates is getting phone calls all the time from English majors writing their senior theses on the novel *them*. She's also getting stacks of postcards picturing cafés on the Left Bank from English majors who've dropped out. As well as tons of manuscripts from unpublished novelists who've never majored in anything. She's canceled all her hairdressing salon's magazine subscriptions. There are manuscripts everywhere, more than she and her customers could ever hope to read or want to, and her phone never stops ringing, and she's had her fill of Pernod-stained postcards.

Dennis can't see what any of this has to do with anthropology, though he does suggest that perhaps she could change *her* name. But she likes her name, she says, and if a name change is in order, how about if the other Joyce Carol Oates changes hers?

As that discussion is going on, Margaret Mead and Claude Lévi-Strauss are getting off a Greyhound bus in front of Lulu's Laundromat. Lulu spots them, unleashes a loud, piercing laugh, and proclaims, You two look just like those weirdos in the posters in the anthropologist's office next door. Whereupon they notice Dennis's sign, saunter over, and go inside, Lulu right behind. Which makes things a little crowded in there.

After introductions and some shuffling about admiring their posters, followed by a round of giggling when Dennis asks what brings them to New Jersey, they're briefed on Ms. Oates's dilemma. A renewed discussion of her name ensues. It gets nowhere.

The hairdresser offers to do Margaret Mead's hair though, which is a mess, and they all go over to her salon, and not only does Ms. Oates do Ms. Mead's hair but Sebastian's too, and she's teasing Claude Lévi-Strauss's when Dennis starts humming one of the Polynesian paddlers' incantations. A few bars along, the hairdresser vanishes. M. Lévi-Strauss puts down the stack of postcards he's been licking Pernod off of while getting his hair teased and goes from mirror to mirror in search of her, but she isn't in any of them. Only his own image, which looks a fright with his sideburns sticking out.

Dennis insists it hadn't been his intention for Ms. Oates to vanish, it was just an obsolete incantation he was humming, and he's as flummoxed as the rest of them. He repeats his insistence and flummoxance to the Saint Plato police after Lulu, giggling piercingly, phones them to report the vanished hairdresser. Nevertheless, he's charged with vanishment and reckless anthropology and kept in a cell overnight. The famous anthropologists spend the night licking Pernod together, Sebastian curled up in a deep sleep in the shampoo sink.

In the morning the police in Lockport, New York, get in touch with Saint Plato's finest in response to a vanished person's bulletin. A disoriented woman has gotten off a bus there claiming she's Joyce Carol Oates, but she doesn't look anything like Joyce Carol Oates, at any rate not the one who grew up in Lockport and became a famous author. And what the fuck is going on down there in New Jersey anyway?

Dennis is ordered to reimburse the hairdresser for her bus ticket. Impressed with his humming, Ms. Mead and M. Lévi-Strauss write up recommendations for him to the top anthropology schools, then hop a Greyhound for Six Flags.

Bring on the roller coasters! M. Lévi-Strauss shouts as they take their seats.

Hush, Claude, Ms. Mead cautions. What will people think?

*

Dennis is accepted at all the schools and given generous stipends and soon he and Sebastian are in Ireland, in FitzSweeney town, and he's buying up all the notebooks he can find to amass data in for his dissertation. He'll research the extinct FitzSweeneys and the extinct Indians both.

But no one in town remembers anything about any FitzSweeneys. Not one story was ever handed down. Not a single FitzSweeney gravestone can be found in the cemetery.

Further, next to nothing is known about the New Jersey Indians. There's no Immigrant Museum. They're not taught about in school. The town library has no books on them. No monument exists concerning any massacre. And boo-all is recollected about the last surviving descendant, who's said to have kept to himself and acted creepy and who was last seen setting off in a canoe with the former Fewest-Freckle Queen.

A tourist goes missing now and then from the former queen's former pub but Dennis gets on well with the cannibal and his family—the cannibal's wife is the new Fewest-Freckle Queen—and he's renting a room from them above the pub. He's been filling notebook after notebook with data ever since he expanded the focus of his research to include whatever he comes across about anything.

At the moment, he and Sebastian are in the pub at one end of the bar, Dennis nursing a glass of FitzSweeney Pale Stout, a notebook open in front of him, pen poised, the cat up on the bar lapping pale stout from a saucer.

Meanwhile, out on FitzSweeney Bay, an outrigger full of prominent Hungarian magicians is foundering.

Foundering, foundered, sunk.

Slurp, gurgle.

Magicians drifting about, clinging to wooden scraps.

But magicians get out of things. Handcuffs, straitjackets,

locked trunks, Budapest. These particular magicians got out of Budapest to attend the umpteenth annual Harry Houdini Symposium on the Sleeping Magician, the uninhabited island off the tip of the FitzSweeney Peninsula that from a distance looks like, well, a sleeping magician.

It was a free afternoon at the symposium and the magicians had taken their outrigger out to sightsee. Harry Houdini's ghost tagged along and was having a grand time of it taking Polaroids.

Alas, singly now and in pairs and in *ménages à trois*, the magicians drift back to the island.

Except for Denísza. She drifts instead to the peninsula itself and washes up onto FitzSweeney Strand.

Denísza sits awhile on the strand, composing herself, lamenting the loss of her shoes in the foundering, then spots a fortune cookie nearby, picks it up, and breaks it apart. Goblops of goulash! she says to herself as she reads the long and extraordinary fortune from inside the cookie. Vhy in Budapezt I not ztay and do tricks vit cards?

She sighs, changes a seagull into a motor scooter, adjusts the mirrors attached to the handlebars, and gazes at her face in them, practicing alluring smiles. Satisfied, she rides the scooter barefoot into FitzSweeney town, right up to the door of Gogaleen Gogginy's former pub, gets off, and changes the scooter back into a seagull. Which prompts a passerby to exclaim, Janey Mack!

Who? Denísza says.

Janey Mack! the passerby exclaims once more. You don't know about *Janey Mack?* It's rivaled in frequency only by *fook!* among expletives in use here in FitzSweeney. Just ask that tall, skinny fellow inside in the pub, the anthropologist, Dennis Dunkle.

Haf he cat?

He haf. I mean, he *has*. That would be Sebastian. They've a room up over the pub. But how'd you do that anyway? Where's the scooter?

Darned if I knowy.

Denísza pushes open the pub door, causing the little bell above it to ring, steps inside, looks around. Fewest-Freckle Queen trophies are on display. As are Dennis and Sebastian. She smiles alluringly at them, strides barefoot to the other end of the bar, asks the cannibal for a glass of fizzy pop, pulls a damp paprika packet from her pocket, and taps its contents into the glass.

Is offizial magizian drink, she informs the mellow old men at her end of the bar. Time passes. She catches Dennis and Sebastian staring. Dennis blushes. Sebastian keeps staring. More time passes. Dennis gulps down the last of his pale stout, tucks his notebook under his arm, takes a deep breath, and makes his way around a knot of tourists over to Denísza. Sebastian trots along the bartop to her.

Tooky youz your zveet times, Denísza says.

Uh, Dennis says. You're barefoot.

I knowy I'm barefoot, she replies.

I'm Dennis Dunkle, he says. I'm an anthropologist. And this is my cat, Sebastian. We've a room up over the pub.

I knowy you're Denniz Dunkle and I knowy you're anzropologizt and your cat's Zebaztian and you live upztairs. Ztop telling me zings already knowy. I'm Denísza. I'm prominent Hungarian magizian. She extends her hand.

They shake and Dennis asks how she knows about him and Sebastian, wonders if it's because she's a magician.

She studies him through several swallows of fizzy pop, puts down her glass, says, Is because pazzerby zaid youz are you and you. Alzo are you prominently menzioned in mine fortune zat vas in fortune cookie I found on FitzZveeney Ztrand. Zpezifically, I am zis very hour to meet tall, zkinny ztranger vit cat in Gogaleen Gogginy's former pub. You are to help fulfill me vit mine deztiny.

I am?

You betcha. But appendix to fortune zays I zhould vatch mine ztep given how your brain's been battered ztarting vit its formative years in Newy Yerzlop.

It says that?

More or lezz.

81

Sebastian is licking paprika from the rim of the glass of fizzy pop. Dennis silently admires Denísza's magical looks— indeed to him she has the presence of an alluring magician— then asks how come she's barefoot. Mine zhoes are at za bottom of FitzZveeney Bay, she says and tells him about the foundering and about her fellow magicians drifting back to the Sleeping Magician.

But the island's uninhabited, he says. There's not even a bed and breakfast on it.

Ve brought from Budapezt our own beds and breakfazts, she says. Not you knowy? Being held on za island as ve zpeak is umpteent annual Harry Houdini Zympozium. Harry vas in Hungary born, but za Zleeping Magizian vas vhere he learned firzt his magic.

It was?

Crozz mine heart. He attended children's magic camp on za island. Za children vould paddle to za mainland to try ztuff out. One day little Harry changed monaztic ruin into paprika pillar.

Into a paprika pillar? Dennis says, opening his notebook.

Oh, close back your zilly notes. Ve go tour za town around, okay?

*

Are you really Hungarian? Dennis asks as they're touring the town around, Sebastian trotting along beside them. I mean, your accent. You don't sound like Zsa Zsa Gabor.

Is because of supprezzed memory of mine unhappy childhood, Denísza says, which is none of your businezzes.

They stop at O'Wu's Fish and Fortune Cookie Take-Away from where Sebastian takes away a fish, Denísza another fizzy pop, Dennis a fortune cookie.

I'm to disregard all previous fortunes, he reports, and be sawed in half by a prominent Hungarian magician named Denísza.

Yipadee-dah-doo! she says. Never anzropologizt before haf I zawed in hafs!

They pause by the garden in front of the priests' house. Former garden. It's all dug up. Large holes are everywhere. Sebastian makes a small hole to pee in. These are Digger Mack's diggings, Dennis explains. Digger's looking for Marie Antoinette's tunnel.

Her vhat?

Her tunnel. It was dug from the harbor up to the priests' house here, and when she escaped from France and sailed to FitzSweeney, she was brought through it, right up to the house. The paparazzi never spotted her.

Zat's full of nonzenzes, Denísza says. In zchool ve ztudied her. Marie Antoinette never ezcaped. Zhe got chopped off at za neck.

That was her stuntwoman who got chopped off at the neck, Dennis says.

Mine bare foot you pull.

I don't. The tourist brochures are very clear. She died of natural causes. Her ghost lives up in the priests' attic. It's been so long, though, she can't remember where the tunnel came out. At first she thought it might have been somewhere around the petunias. But Digger had no luck around the petunias.

Za priezts let him dig? Juzt like zat?

Well, he's sort of special to them. His mother was their housekeeper. Tourists are always photographing each other down the street there in front of her grotto. It honors her for giving birth to him as a virgin.

How extrooordinny! Vhat does zat make Digger?

Digger's just Digger. He's a bit simpleminded. But it's a tradition here to exclaim his mother's name, Janey Mack, whenever anyone feels like it.

Of courze! Earlier minezelf heard I her name exclaimed.

You can count on an exclamation or two at any given hour. There'll be a chorus of them when Digger finds the tunnel. His progress is followed closely. Packets of dirt from the holes are sold in the pubs. The publicans bless the dirt and write *FitzSweeney Holy Dirt* on the packets. I've been collecting them, a packet from each pub. Let's go back. They're in the room. I'll show them to you.

If you muzt, Denísza says. But no funny businezzes!

As they start to retrace their steps, an Elvis Presley song floats down from an open window in the attic of the priests' house. It's *Don't Be Cruel* with harp accompaniment. Sebastian pauses, looks up to the window, a forepaw raised, listening.

Elviz! Denísza says. Za king! Marie Antoinette haf radio on. Or phonograph.

No radio, Dennis says. No phonograph. That's *live* from the attic. Elvis is singing and Marie Antoinette is accompanying him on her harp. They live in sin up there. Their ghosts do.

Alzo Elviz lives in attic? His ghost? Vit hers? In zin? Zat's one for za tabloids.

Maybe. But it's common knowledge here. Digger was Elvis's biggest fan in FitzSweeney. He wrote to him, inviting him to visit the town, said that if he disguised himself as a priest, he could stay in the priests' house for free. But Elvis never answered the letter. Then he died.

Denísza nods. Outriggers flew haf mazt za flags up and down za Danube.

Digger was half-mast too, Dennis says. Then Elvis showed up.

In za flezh?

Not exactly in the flesh anymore, no, but he was wearing a priest's cloak and strumming his Gibson in front of the grotto. Digger ran into him there and exclaimed *Janey Mack!* so loud he could be heard from one end of FitzSweeney to the other. Even he exclaims his mother's name when it's called for.

They've reached Dennis's and Sebastian's room. Notebooks are everywhere—all over the floor, the bed, on tables and chairs. Dennis steps over and around them to a dresser, a pile of packets on it of FitzSweeney Holy Dirt. He starts gathering up the packets to show to Denísza.

Put down zose zilly packets, she says. Tell me vhat happened next vit za ghozts.

Uh, well, what happened next was Elvis's ghost was given a room in the priests' house and, skulking around one afternoon, he ran into Marie Antoinette's ghost on the stairs. In no time he was up in the attic singing love songs to her and

84

they became an item. They lived quietly in the attic. Happily. She was on the pill so no worries. But the priests found out about her pills and confiscated them and now she's pregnant. The baby's almost due.

Is heir to za zrone!

Um, because her mother was Queen of Hungary?

Bingo! Zey muzt get zemzelfs to Budapezt zo born baby can be coronated!

But they like FitzSweeney. They want to build a house here.

Zey von't be building zquat.

Huh?

Tonight I make FitzZveeney dizappear.

Dennis stares at her. Tonight you—? Why?

Because mine fortune zays I do. Didn't I menzion zat part of it?

Uh, no. You can really make the town disappear?

Prominent magizians can make anyzing dizappear. I do it in mine zleep.

Maybe the town will still be somewhere?

Maybe not. Entirely I'm to do it avay.

What about me? What about Sebastian?

You and your cat get tranzported to za Zleeping Magizian and vhen is ready our new boat, ve outrigger you back vit uz to Budapezt.

My notebooks too! My notebooks must get transported and outriggered too!

Zere von't be room! Tonight ve zleep and vhen in morning ve vake, pub is toazted, upztairs here is toazted, town is toazted, ve are on Zleeping Magizian. You are handzhaking Harry Houdini, Zebaztian is lapzitting him. Period. Your tootbruzh I borrow now. And nightzhirt.

But my notebooks!

Yaney Mack! Tootbruzh and nightzhirt please!

You're sleeping here?

Zelibately. Bed haf two zides, no? As for za notebooks on it, vatch! Denísza waves her hand at them and they go poof. As for rezt of za notebooks, vatch again! She waves her hand around the room and the remaining notebooks go poof.

85

Sebastian has run under the bed. Now, for lazt time: Tootbruzh and nightzhirt!

Tears trickle down Dennis's face. All my amassed data, all gone poof, he whimpers. He whimpers on as he gets his toothbrush for her and a t-shirt that says *Proud to Be from Saint Plato.*

Denísza ignores the whimpering and soon enough both of them are in bed, at opposite edges, Denísza in Dennis's adequately long t-shirt calmly anticipating what's ahead, Dennis in his pajamas, morose. She looks over at him, smiles unseductively, says, C'mon, let's znuggle, slides toward him. Sebastian comes out from under the bed and snuggles between them.

Now ve lay uz down to zleep, Denísza prays. All zis go poof before ve vake, or mine magic be one big fake.

*

Morning.

Denísza stretches, yawns, opens her eyes, looks around. Packets of FitzSweeney Holy Dirt are scattered about. But about where? It's not the room they went to sleep in, it wouldn't be, that's gone poof. But they can't be on the Sleeping Magician either, there are no rooms on the Sleeping Magician.

Vhere za fooklop are ve? Denísza wants to know, shaking Dennis awake.

He gets up, creeps over to the window, looks down at the street below, gasps.

Oh-oh, Denísza says. I zink I knowy. Ve're in Newy Yerzlop, aren't ve? Zis vas your bedroom, vasn't it?

It was once, Dennis says. But how did this happen?

Denísza in a small voice: I zcrewied up.

Sebastian opens an eye, closes it.

I hate to bring this up, Dennis says, but I *am* supposed to help you fulfill your destiny. Maybe you belong here.

Za fooklop I do! Vhere is batroom?

Batroom? Oh.

Dennis points.

Denísza collects the packets of holy dirt, takes them into the bathroom, fills the bathtub, empties packet after packet into the water.

Dennis has followed in his pajamas. Why are you doing that? he asks.

Is Hail Mária, she says, climbing into the tub, still wearing the Saint Plato shirt. You get in too.

Fully awake now, Sebastian ambles into the bathroom himself, hops up onto the rim of the tub, and stares at them.

They sit in silence for a long time in the muddy water, getting muddy. And muddier.

Zo much for Hail Mária, Denísza says finally. Apparently ve're ztaying. Ve climb out now and vazh off za mud.

*

Molly Minnelli makes them breakfast. And lunch. And supper.

That night a jug of Veezlaat is uncorked and the three of them end up in bed together. Sebastian sits at the foot of the bed and stares.

The next morning Molly is smiling. Denísza is aghast. Dennis is confused. Sebastian is hungry.

*

Without his notebooks, without his amassed data, Dennis is unable to write his dissertation. He reopens the storefront on Main Street, but business is slow. When Denísza is appointed Prominent Professor of Magic at the college, he and Sebastian become magician's assistants. During magic shows in Fedankgo Auditorium, she gleefully saws Dennis in half. Sebastian pulls rabbits out of hats and chases them around the auditorium.

One day an envelope of Polaroids arrives in the mail. There's a Polaroid of an empty space where FitzSweeney town used to be. There's a Polaroid of Marie Antoinette and Elvis proudly holding up an infant wearing a crown in front of

Wubik's Goulash and Fortune Cookie Take-Away in Budapest. There's one of Digger Mack sitting on a mound of dirt next to a big hole in China. And there are a bunch of very steamy ones of Dennis and Denísza and Molly in bed together in various positions *in flagrante delicto*.

Denísza gasps, aghast all over again.

Off her game, when next she saws Dennis in half, he's shortened considerably. Oh zzzzzzzzzhit! she says and changes herself into a seagull and flutters hurriedly out of town.

Sebastian sticks by Dennis and becomes a service cat.

Molly has the steamy Polaroids blown up to life-size and affixes them to her bedroom walls and ceiling.

# SEVEN

When Dennis is only a few weeks old, his mother is eaten by a lion. She's swinging in a hammock, raptly tallying proceeds from a ponzi scheme, when the lion pounces. It's believed to have escaped from a traveling circus. Or a zoo. Or a movie. It's last seen swimming upstream in Saint Plato Creek. Or downstream. Or in the high school pool. Accounts vary.

Gladys Dunkle duly noted in Dennis's baby book her disappointment with his gender. She also wrote down a diabolical plan to call him Denise. Otherwise she left behind no thoughts of him. In this particular world, orphaned, he's adopted by Mrs. Olé who cremates the baby book in her outdoor grill. He becomes Dennis Olé.

Mrs. Olé had married Señor Olé instead of Billy Baker whose proposals she'd rejected again and again. Billy'd had a crush on her for years. But he was no bullfighter. He was a carpenter. And she was into bullfighters. Señor Olé was a matador who'd been trampled by a bull in Fedankgo's Bullring. He wasn't her first choice among bullfighters. Fergolo Fedankgo was *numero uno*. Fergolo, however, had been pressured into an arranged marriage with a spoiled bull-breeding heiress from Cape May. He did remain available illicitly.

Señor Olé was a familiar sight around town, rolling his wheelchair all the way to the First Bank of Saint Plato to cash his bullfighter disability checks, and rolling it all the way the other way to Lock No. 1 on Saint Plato Creek where he managed as best he could as a part-time disabled assistant locktender. Until, that is, he went showing off on the locktending catwalk one day, swiveling about, attempting a *serpentina*, and he and his wheelchair swiveled out of control and plunged onto the deck of a barge that had become stuck in the lock.

Dennis's mother hadn't been eaten by the lion yet. Dennis hadn't been born yet. But it was the same day Mrs. Olé had sex with Babe Ruth and switched her sports interests from bullfighting to baseball.

89

The Babe happened to be traveling on the very barge that got stuck and, as chance would have it, it got stuck just as Mrs. Olé was dropping off a bullburger for Señor Olé's lunch. The disabled señor expected it would take all afternoon to free the boat, especially since he was in no hurry, contemplating as he'd been all morning the execution of that *serpentina,* a vaunted maneuver from his glory days in the bullring, stuck barge be damned.

Bullfighting was the pastime of record in New Jersey then, the only state without a baseball team of any sort, and Babe Ruth, on a promotional tour for the game, was out to change that. Not one to pass up an opportunity, he cranked up the barge's Victrola, put on T*ake Me Out to the Ballgame,* swaggered out onto the deck with his favorite bat and a bucket of balls, hitched up his trousers, and began hitting fungoes out onto Creek Street.

A baseball whizzed past Mrs. Olé as she was leaving the lock and she turned and spotted the Babe holding what she thought might be a new kind of *banderilla.*

What was with the ball? she shouted at him. Aren't you a bullfighter?

Hell, no! he shouted back. I'm a famous baseball player. Watch! He tossed another ball into the air and whacked it with his bat—what Mrs. Olé had thought might have been a *banderilla*—and the ball sailed toward her, bouncing right in front of her.

She caught it on the bounce barehanded and said, Fancy that!

You're a natural, Babe Ruth shouted.

Come ashore, why don't you, she yelled. I'll give you a tour of the town.

They got no farther than her house and were well into what they were into when Señor Olé and his wheelchair swiveled and plunged.

*

It was becoming quite a homestand. The previous weekend

Señor Olé had weekend duty at the lock and Mrs. Olé and Fergolo Fedankgo had torrid sex.

She and Fergolo had been an item ever since high school when he was captain of Saint Plato Central High's bullfighting team. The Fedankgo family was up to its ears in bulls and, at bull-running time, when the bulls were run through the streets of Saint Plato, the future Mrs. Olé would run along briefly with the migrant bull-runners up from Florida, then slip off to meet Fergolo in one of the vacated bull sheds and go at it. Other times, other places. They didn't let up even after his marriage to the spoiled bull-breeding heiress from Cape May. Nor after Mrs. Olé's marriage on the rebound to Señor Olé, whose capacity for sex seemed understandably diminished.

With a broken heart, Billy Baker chucked his carpentry tools into the creek, flipped a coin, and boarded a bus for a state where everyone speaks with a drawl. He began speaking with a drawl himself and got into politics.

\*

Mrs. Olé might not have invited Babe Ruth ashore if she hadn't been so upset with Fergolo. Or she might have. You never know.

What upset her so much was that Fergolo was pressing to take a breather from their torrid sex. The spoiled heiress was getting suspicious. A few torrid weekends ago, for example, he was supposed to have been inspecting free-range bulls out on the barrier islands. But he didn't bring home a single barrier island souvenir, only a lot of dog hairs on his clothes from the Olés' bulldog. The heiress didn't buy his explanation that they were baby bull hairs.

That same weekend, Señor Olé was supposed to have been attending a convention up in Upper Saddle River for part-time disabled assistant locktenders. But there had been no convention for part-time disabled assistant locktenders that particular weekend up in Upper Saddle River or anywhere else. Rather, he'd been shacked up the whole weekend with a teller from the First Bank of Saint Plato in a motel cabin over near Asbury Park.

He confessed this indiscretion, and a bunch more, to Mrs. Olé in the ER at Saint Plato General some hours after his plunge onto the deck of the barge and her plunge into bed with the Babe. Down to his last beeps on the heart monitor before meeting his maker, Señor Olé was of no mind to hedge on the truth.

I couldn't keep my pants on around the tellers, he told her. The way they would lean out their little windows and smile seductively and say *Olé!* He'd slept with every one of them at the First Bank, rendezvousing with several right in the safe deposit vault. And there were offspring, though he ran out of beeps before he could get to that.

You sure had me fooled, Mrs. Olé said as he beeped out, not troubling him a whit about Fergolo or the Babe. Fergolo soon met his maker as well, the heiress shoving him in front of a streetful of stampeding bulls. The widowed Mrs. Olé was totally into baseball by then.

*

She never tells Dennis he's adopted. She tells him she's his mother and Babe Ruth's his father. Bullfighting posters that once covered the walls of the house have been postered over with baseball posters. The bulldog refuses to fetch baseballs and is dropped off at the bank. Dennis is home-schooled, mostly in baseball's fundamentals. None of it takes. The new bat, ball, and glove he's given for his tenth birthday he trades for an old guitar.

Mrs. Olé keeps hoping. At her urging, in high school, Dennis tries out for Saint Plato Central's baseball team, the sport now big in New Jersey. But concepts such as fair ball versus foul and which way to run the bases escape him. He mostly strikes out and flubs easy catches and goes and strums his guitar behind the backstop where a large fluffy white cat hangs out. Baseball is beyond Dennis's pale.

War is also beyond his pale. After an eternity of home schooling and an unstimulating year of community college,

92

Vietnam heats up and he gets his draft notice. Which gets him hitchhiking to Canada with his guitar. Anywhere in Canada will do, and after a few short rides, one comes along that's going to Maine. So Dennis goes to Maine and stows away on a ferry to Nova Scotia.

It's not long before he's strumming away and singing anti-war songs in a coffeehouse in Halifax and falling head over heels for Denisita, a svelte exchange waitress from the Dominican Republic whose uncles are famous baseball umpires there. Once she learns Dennis's father is Babe Ruth, she's head over heels too.

He does warn her of his difficulties with baseball, of his lack of skills, and that he hardly understands the game. Not to mention Spanish.

Just hoot, root, and toot for the home team in *inglés,* Denisita advises. He can't help but hoot, root, and toot around her and he composes incoherent baseball ballads to add to his repertoire. They wed in the coffeehouse. Within a year Denisita gives birth to triplet girls and names them Georgie and Hermanie and Ruthie.

All at once three times a father, Dennis searches for a day job and finds one that gives him barely time for a catnap between getting home late at night from the coffeehouse and rising before dawn to sort the mail he will trudge through snow and sleet and freezing rain to deliver in Halifax.

Reviving her agenda, the elder Mrs. Olé, Granny Olé as she's now known, packs a giant sports bag with bats, balls, and gloves and travels up from New Jersey. She and Denisita start playing catch with Georgie and Hermanie and Ruthie when they can barely walk. Soon they're pitching batting practice to them and playing pepper with them and hitting fungoes for them to shag. Dennis tries to join in but he's so incompetent he's told to bugger off, to go compose a few more incoherent ballads if he wouldn't mind.

When amnesty is announced for those who fled to Canada during Vietnam, Dennis composes a ballad that begins:

> *Neither snow nor sleet nor freezing rain*
> *could get me to return to the New Jersey plain.*

Odds are it would go unnoticed except a local television cameraman happens to be in the coffeehouse nursing a triple espresso after a slow news day when Dennis is performing it in his mail carrier's uniform. It makes the late night news all over North America, then the morning shows.

Though sympathetic, the post office suspends him, then thinks better of it and dismisses him. South of the border, the CIA starts a Dennis Olé file. Amnesty in his case is revoked.

*

Denisita and Granny Olé are phenomenal coaches, especially considering how short the baseball season is in Halifax. When Georgie and Hermanie and Ruthie come of age, they dress them as boys and take them to spring training in Florida.

New Jersey has long since outlawed bullfighting. And the spoiled bull-breeding heiress, sent to prison for offing Fergolo, has long since bribed her way out and is back in Cape May inventing her memoirs. Saint Plato, meanwhile, has grown exponentially into a large city and has been awarded an expansion franchise in the American League. This will be its first season. Fedankgo's Bullring has been converted into Fedankgo Field, home of the Saint Plato Plates. Baseball rules. With a spring roster of has-beens from the expansion draft, the team's looking for good young prospects.

Not only are the triplets half-Dominican, Denisita tells the Plates' GM.

They're also one-quarter-Babe-Ruth, Granny adds.

They go through drills and are so adept at everything that they're signed on the spot. They're better than prospects. *George* and *Herman* and *Rutherford* Olé are in the Plates' starting lineup on opening day at Fedankgo Field.

Denisita and Granny and Dennis fly down from Halifax for the game, himself wearing a disguise and studying a baseball primer. As if there isn't enough excitement when they get off the plane at Saint Plato International, Billy Baker, now a contender in the presidential primaries and arriving back in his hometown to throw out the first ball, accidentally smack-dabs into Dennis. Things quickly get out of hand and the potential future president is sitting in a jail cell when it comes time to throw out that ball.

The smack-dab knocked off Dennis's wig and false nose, and Billy Baker suddenly was face to face with a face that had been singing on the late night news and the morning shows that neither snow nor sleet nor freezing rain could get it to return to the New Jersey plain. The contender was quite beside himself and drawled incoherently. Frustrated, flailing at the air, he unwittingly goosed Granny, the woman who years earlier had broken his heart. She screamed. Which brought the airport police on the double. They didn't believe he was who he was — since when would a potential future president who grew up in Saint Plato and was returning to throw out the first ball on opening day go around goosing people at the airport?

With Billy Baker's whereabouts unaccounted for, the triplets get to throw out the first three balls. In the game, they smack several triples each and participate in a triple play. At the seventh inning stretch, when Dennis stands with the crowd to sing *When the Plates Go Marching In*, his reaffixed wig and false nose are again knocked off and he's spotted by CIA operatives in the stands. They start a wave to create a diversion, pluck Dennis from his seat, rush him to the airport, and airmail him to a black site.

By the time Billy Baker's Billy Bakerness is verified downtown at the jail, the game is on the wane. The jailer suggests that if he hurries, he might make it to Fedankgo Field in time to throw out the last ball. Which he thinks a splendid idea. The matter of the goosing is expunged from the police records. The Plates win handily but Billy Baker gets to the field too late to throw out any ball.

*

Believing that Dennis was swept away by the wave, Denisita and Granny return to Halifax and sweep him from their thoughts. They concentrate on following the exploits of George and Herman and Rutherford in the newspapers and when the Plates are playing in the game of the week on television. The talk of the sports world, the triplets are considered shoo-ins for joint Rookies of the Year if not Most Valuable Players.

But after the opener they had let their hair down and become Georgie and Hermanie and Ruthie that night and met a fellow with a drawl at Fedankgo's Discotheque and before long started having morning sickness, all three of them. That fellow was Billy Baker, hardly enjoying his Veezlaat at the bar, wallowing as he was in his disappointment over arriving at a deserted Fedankgo Field. But he did a triple-take as the triplets walked up to the bar and an instant later began drawling his heart out. He woke in the morning in Fedankgo Towers, in a penthouse suite billed to his credit card. The triplets, whoever they were, were gone.

In August Billy Baker is nominated to head his party's ticket and by September George and Herman and Rutherford start to show. Callers on sports radio talk shows are saying it doesn't look like beer bellies.

The Plates have clinched first place in their division but before the month is out, the truth is out. A pregnant Georgie Olé and a pregnant Hermanie Olé and a pregnant Ruthie Olé are on the cover of *Sports Illustrated*. They're suspended forever. Or, the baseball commissioner rules, until they get a sex change. Billy Baker's central role is exposed, the goosing too, and he's replaced on the ticket.

Dang it! he drawls over and over to himself. Doesn't my libidinousness count for anything?

His drawl was kinda cute, Georgie tells the *Daily Banner*.

But if we had known it was he who goosed our grandmother, Hermanie adds, he wouldn't have gotten to first base.

And no way we're getting a sex change, Ruthie makes clear.

It's the curse of the Bambino all over again, the Plates' GM laments when the team falls flat in the playoffs without the triplets in the lineup.

Liberal baseball teams the world over besiege Georgie and Hermanie and Ruthie, the Plovdiv Plovs in the Bulgarian Unisex League making the best offer. The team pays them top *lev* and provides a villa on the River Maritsa and throws in a maternity wing. In which wing the births occur, three more sets of triplets, nine babies altogether, a whole baseball team someday, girls and boys both.

Georgie and her sisters successfully petition the Bulgarian courts to deny a mouthy Billy Baker visiting rights, bragging rights, and all other rights. Dang it! he drawls anew. Craving a political comeback and the opportunity thereby to impose sanctions on Bulgaria, he buys a minor league baseball team with funds siphoned from somewhere they shouldn't be and practices throwing out first balls, practices so hard he wrecks his arm and needs Tommy John surgery. He petitions unsuccessfully to have it renamed *Billy Baker surgery.*

Dennis remains renditioned.

*

Meanwhile, casting about for an Emmy in broadcast journalism, *29 Minutes* dispatches an entire journalism class to collect DNA samples from Babe Ruth's bat and Señor Olé's wheelchair and Fergolo Fedankgo's cape and Dennis's false nose and what have you and the program concludes, startlingly, that Babe Ruth is not Dennis's father. Nor is anyone else. Nor therefore are Georgie, Hermanie, and Ruthie descendants of the Babe. Granny Olé is not Dennis's mother either.

Well, fuck, Denisita says when told of the findings.

Babe who? Granny asks, slumped in her recliner in a nursing home after a stroke.

But *29 Minutes* loses out in the Emmy voting to *News at 6* which, at the contest deadline, airs a special revealing that Billy Baker is not the father of any of the triplets' triplets. Their actual father, *News at 6* reports, is a peanut vendor at Fedankgo Field.

*

Dreams of a talented Olé Nine in the Plovs' lineup together are dashed when one of the nine elects to study for the

97

priesthood. She goes on to become the first pope whose father is a peanut vendor and makes the cover of *Sports Illustrated* herself, blessing baseballs for the Bulgarian Unisex League's All-Star Game.

Dennis is allowed to listen to play-by-plays on a short wave boom box at the black site, but the broadcasts are in Bulgarian and he doesn't understand a word. He's also given an old guitar for recreational use but it has no strings. It's long been determined that he's harmless, that it was a colossal mistake renditioning him. Yet to let him go and admit the kidnapping and, well, that he was leaned on and that he's been confined since and that the guitar they gave him has no strings, such admissions would make the agency look bad. And who needs that?

# EIGHT

Get this: Twice Dennis Dunkle marries Lola Tcholar, the sensual potentate of the Veezlaat empire. Both times it's her second marriage, his first. We're talking two worlds here. In both of them, Dennis is again orphaned early on when his mother is eaten by a lion. In one world, Mrs. Olé down the street isn't into orphans and he's raised by agnostic missionaries. In the other world, no one at all is into orphans and he grows up in the Saint Plato Orphanage, a ward of the State of New Jersey. A Denise or two show up in both worlds. But Lola and her Veezlaat come first.

They deserve a novel of their own, Lola and her Veezlaat, and somewhere out there perhaps it's been written. Or it will be. In this one, they'll have only these few pages following.

It was Lola's grandmother, Zoltána Tcholar, who originally concocted Veezlaat. Our Lady of Saint Plato Pale Ale was then and still is the suds of choice in town. But among the hard stuff it's Veezlaat—the grog that makes men weep at the moon and swoon over marigolds, that makes women melt in the moonlight and in every other kind of light and in no light at all.

As a slip of a girl barely off the boat from the old country, Zoltána Tcholar skipped her first day of school, gathered a profusion of aromatic weeds from along the Saint Plato & Western tracks at the edge of town, shoplifted a chemistry set from the Five-and-Dime, and set about distilling the grog. She named it after her Uncle Veezlaat who missed the boat. Wasting nothing, she used the roots, stems, leaves, and flowers of the weeds, and any insects caught up in the gathering. In the early going, Zoltána dispensed it in paper cups from her mother's goulash stand in front of their house. It was an instant smash in the neighborhood, the line of customers often circling the block.

The weeds kept profusing and so did the luscious and gusty, very high proof, very illegal Veezlaat. The Roaring

Twenties and Prohibition in New Jersey would not have been the same without it. The Tcholars could hardly launder the proceeds fast enough. After Prohibition, it remained illegal and sales kept getting better and better. Deliveries that began humbly by bicycle progressed to horse and cart, then small trucks, then big trucks, and much later in one of the worlds, thanks to Dennis, a helicopter.

Long before there was a Dennis or a Lola, when Zoltána came of age she acquired from a Sears catalog a mail-order hunk she named Stud. She herself was never abusive toward Stud, but he was constantly being battered and bruised by the barrels and jugs of Veezlaat he kept bumping into and tripping over around the house. Zoltána was making the grog and aging it everywhere inside, from basement to attic, as well as on the porch and in the garage and out back in the tool shed.

Stud never healed properly and for good until Zoltána passed the torch to their daughter, Izabella, an astute businesswoman who buncoed the First Bank of Saint Plato's president one Sadie Hawkins Day and would become Lola Tcholar's unwed mother and the recipient of a most generous skimming of bank funds. The skimming bankrolled a state-of-the-art distillery built under wraps nearby the now abandoned Saint Plato & Western tracks. During construction, not one weed in the whole profusion of weeds was allowed to be disturbed. Izabella christened the place an environmental start-up for the protection of endangered flora.

Looking out on the flora from the top floor of the distillery was Lola's day nursery, giving the child an early introduction, you might say, to the business. Later, as a drop-dead gorgeous sophomore at Saint Plato Central High, she began taking a more active role. She brought a thermos of Veezlaat to school one day and sipped a bit of it during a boring biology class and a bit more during a boring study hall and invited Father Prendergast, the drop-dead Adonis of a stutter-prone Religions of the World teacher, to meet her out under the football-field bleachers to share what was left. An assistant pastor at the upstart Parish of a Saint To Be Named Later, Father Prendergast didn't stutter once, silently, reverently sipping from the thermos and weeping at Lola's beauty. For her part, she melted.

In the weeks that followed, the two of them inwardly looked back with drop-dead exuberance at their bleachers tête-à-tête. Outwardly they played it cool, merely winking at each other when passing in the halls. Then Lola found out she was you know what. The priest had considered their liaison a miracle—Adonis or not, as a celibate clergyman with a stutter, he'd been lucky to wrangle an occasional hank or pank with a dour housekeeper. Now he was confronted with an altogether more complicated miracle.

Izabella envisioned a number of advantages to marriage for her underage daughter. Lola thought it would be a hoot. Negotiations took place and the gleeful priest agreed to bestow enough indulgences for all the Tcholars to ascend directly into heaven when their times came. He also consented to promoting Veezlaat in ecclesiastical circles, a hitherto untapped market.

A barge captain on a layover on Saint Plato Creek was cajoled with a number of jugs of the grog into performing the ceremony in secret on his barge before turning the boat over to the bride and groom for a short but wildly passionate honeymoon. No one knew. Not the regulars at the diner. Not the saloon crowd. No one.

The newlyweds then stayed discreetly apart. Lola gave birth the following summer at a Kittatinny Mountains chalet for affluent Hungarians with better-left-unexplained dilemmas, a boy who howled a lot. Father Prendergast baptized the howler in the birdbath behind the chalet and he was raised there, supported by a generous Veezlaat endowment. Sipping the grog himself, he became quieter and in time quite proficient at winter sports, winning a modest assortment of Olympic medals for Hungary.

But that was much later. When Lola returned to school in the fall, she and the priest began tête-à-tête-ing away, with prophylactic precautions now and always a thermos of Veezlaat. Living together wasn't feasible, but they did talk of coming out from under the bleachers once she'd finished high school and he'd reached the milestone of ten years in the priesthood—his *aluminum jubilee,* he liked to call it.

In other extracurricular activity, Lola made the cheerleading squad and soon was leading chants of *Let's Go, Hedgehogs* at pep rallies and cartwheeling about at the football games themselves, ravishing in her pink and gold outfit. But most eyes were drawn to Father Prendergast, prancing jollily along the sidelines in his pink ascot and gold denims, urging the Hedgehogs on with mysterious stutterings in Latin or Hungarian or proto-Prendergastian, take your pick. His antics, it was believed, were turning certain defeat into victory week after week.

In the winter the cheerleaders plied the school's hockey rink and so did Father Prendergast, although the hockey team remained a model of mediocrity. The prancing came to an abrupt end when he slipped on the ice during a second intermission and was run over by a Zamboni, decidedly short of his aluminum jubilee. The third period was cancelled and his body was chipped free and removed to the morgue. Lola finished high school at home, more or less in mourning, Izabella providing a private tutor said to be morally impeccable. Lola suspected he was a eunuch.

The hockey team was disbanded but Father Prendergast was invoked unabashedly at football pep rallies the following season—a cheer comprised of stutters had been composed for the rallies—and the football team went undefeated again. So unaccountable were the results that they were elevated to miracle status and the Parish of a Saint To Be Named Later became Blesséd Prendergast Parish. The blesséd one's remains were exhumed and encased in the altar of the church.

*

Some years later, returning from a bash at a Club Veezlaat she'd just opened on the Danube—the Veezlaat empire now all hers, her mother having cashed in her indulgences and ascended into heaven—Lola grabbed a cab to Teterboro from the Newark airport and dashed across the tarmac at the airfield there to a commuter helicopter about to depart for Saint Plato. Captain Dennis Dunkle was at the controls.

Helicopter pilot during Vietnam though he never got there, amateur practitioner of ancient poetic forms, speaker of foreign tongues spoken only on faraway missionary islands, he awkwardly helped her aboard. Lola found his awkwardness sexy. She wanted him.

Dennis knew her only by reputation. Now he would become part of that reputation and experience unprecedented erotic heights and add Hungarian to his list of tongues. He was also an immense asset to the empire, flying helicoptersful of the grog to one new destination after another.

They'd recited their marriage vows in the midst of the profusion of weeds in front of the distillery, an aromatic outdoor ceremony, and they might have aromatically renewed their vows ever after except that by a certain age Dennis was no longer holding his Veezlaat well, no longer weeping and swooning. He also was no longer flying, ending his usefulness as a distributor of the grog. Mistaking the Saint Plato Rec Center's pool for a helipad was what did it. There was no loss of life. But much grog spilled from the broken jugs. Word quickly spread and a frenzied horde guzzled the pool dry.

*

Rejected, divorced, alone, Dennis submerged himself into ineptly perfecting inept imitations he'd been writing of ghazals, a form of ancient Persian poetry he'd chanced upon in an anthology from the bargain table at Fedankgo's Used Books. A few of his imitations were published and that led to his teaching a basic poetry course at the Rec Center, fantasizing that a sensual potential poetess would enroll. No luck there. But he kept devising courses, keeping his fantasies alive.

This year he's teaching Poetic Hungarian, Tuesdays and Thursdays, 7 to 8:30 p.m., just down the hall from Intermediate Hip-Hop. Five women have signed up, a dream come true. If only. One is a mean-looking nun from Blesséd Prendergast Parish. They go south from there. Except for Denise Pritchett—

or Pratchett, Dennis can never remember which—who's a knockout. Except, as she emphasizes when introductions are made at the first class, she's born again. And therefore assuredly unavailable, gleams of proselytizing in Hungarian odes in her eyes.

Last year Dennis taught Plains Indian Smoke-Signal Poetry, a bit of a stretch but he'd been doing some research on smoke signals and he winged it. Indeed poetic puffs of smoke began wafting skyward weekly from the Rec Center's soccer field, sent aloft by the three women in the course—the identical twin spinsters and coincidentally another Denise, also a knockout, Denise Fedankgo. She smoke-signaled couplets that rhymed stuff like *man oh man* and *bam bam*. Her cell phone played the theme from *The Sopranos*.

Danger lurked, but Dennis was intrigued. He almost invited her for coffee after the twins died. Weeks earlier the sisters had simultaneously sent identical impromptu limericks up in smoke while crouched on opposite sides of the soccer field from each other. But then they had simultaneous identical minor surgeries followed by simultaneous identical major complications and that was all they wrote.

Dennis and Denise attempted memorial smoke signals but it was windy that afternoon and he was one blown-out match away from suggesting they give up and head for the diner for memorial cups of Supremo when she checked her watch, spewed an obscenity, muttered she was late, it was her turn to go rub out someone, and dashed off. She didn't return. Next class, only a large fluffy white cat showed up, at a distance. The remaining classes were cancelled. Never getting off the ground was a plan Dennis had to self-publish a video of smoke-signal sonnets.

Leading up to Poetic Hungarian, more of his ghazals appeared in print. He'd modestly concede, however, that his success likely was due to his use of Hungarian words in the refrains, poetry editors finding the Hungarian incomprehensible and concluding it must be esoteric.

He'd learned the language from Lola in bed initially. Her range of vocabulary and grammatical structure while they

104

were doing it was astonishing. His plan at the first class was to break the ice by mentioning what Lola mentioned their first night together, that the Hungarian word *nem* means both *sex* and *no*. Except with a nun and a born-again in the front row, he thought better of it.

*

Dennis also thinks better of rejecting Molly Minnelli's attempts to get him to join Poets on the Prowl. It's been ages since Lola bailed, she keeps reminding him. Do something! And so, when it appears certain that no prospects are enrolled in Poetic Hungarian, just as nothing panned out in Smoke Signals, he gives in and, prowling one day, comes upon *Passionate Pennsylvania Poetess*. This is exciting.

*Dear PPP,* he writes in the message box, his heart beating very fast. *I too am full of P's. I'm passionate and I write lots of poetry and I write first in pencil. See my set of Poly Ghazals in the latest issue of Persian Platypod. Right now I'm teaching Poetic Hungarian. I also know Papuan and Polynesian and a pidgin from when my missionary foster parents were spreading agnosticism in the Pacific. You're very pretty in your photo. Propitiously, Dennis.*

One, two, three days go by without a response. Then, Zowie! Which, Dennis claims, is the same in Hungarian: *Zowie!*

*Propitiously?* the poetess writes back. *Are you for real? I hope so. I love your Poly Ghazals, the refrains are so esoteric! See my Parsing Passion poem in the August Punxsutawney Pentameter. I like your photo too. Pentametrically, Priscilla.*

Pentametric Priscilla! Dennis is enchanted. He changes *Priscilla* to the Hungarian, however, and calls her *Piroska* from then on.

Messages go back and forth. Soon they are on the phone every night. Dennis writes love ghazal after love ghazal to Piroska. He reads them over the phone to her. He reads them to his Hungarian class too.

Piroska begins picking up Hungarian. Their phone conversations start and end like this: *Szeretlek, Piroska. Szeretlek, Dennis.* I love you, Piroska. I love you, Dennis. They talk of meeting as soon as his course is over.

Ah, but trouble brews. Knockout born-again Denise Pritchett/Pratchett has been turned on by the love ghazals Dennis has been reading to the class. She lingers after class one night and coos that they should go for a drink. She can always get born again tomorrow again. Dennis is torn. But she's right next to him, breathing on him. He can smell her lipstick. Piroska is in Pennsylvania and still unmet. He'll phone her later.

*Nem probléma,* Dennis tells Denise Pritchett/Pratchett. They go in separate cars to Fedankgo's Saloon, park behind the place, come in through the rear door, and sit in a booth in back. Good thing. It turns out that Denise has a sometimes boyfriend. He begged off a date with her tonight. And he's up at the bar, putting the make on a buxom woman with a loud piercing laugh—Lulu, the proprietor of Lulu's Laundromat. Or is Lulu putting the make on him?

Enraged either way, Denise stomps up to the bar, grabs Lulu by her buxomness, and yanks her off her barstool. So much for a good thing. Dennis knows he should vanish into the night but instead heads to the bar himself, intent on calming the situation. Lulu kicks him in the balls. Denise kicks her sometimes boyfriend in the balls. When the police arrive, she and Lulu are trying to yank each other's hair out and the two men are writhing on the floor. All four of them are arrested on multiple counts of being morons.

*

Back in Pennsylvania, passionate Piroska can hardly wait another night for Dennis's course to end. When he hasn't called yet himself, she phones him at home and leaves a message imploring him to come spend the weekend with her. They will meet at last and have *nem!* Lots and lots of *nem!* Detained by the police, Dennis never gets home to hear the message until it's too late.

Upset about him not calling back, Piroska becomes Priscilla again, prowls online until she comes upon a poetic swami in

Swarthmore, and that is that. She leaves another message for Dennis, cancelling her weekend invitation, mentioning that she's converting to Hinduism, and adding: *Én ne szeret már.* I don't love you anymore. Her last words ever of Hungarian.

Charges against the Saloon Four are reduced to a single count each of public witlessness. Compulsory brain scans are ordered and they pay fines and are released. That's in the morning. Dennis hobbles home, still smarting from the kick, and listens to Piroska's messages. *Nem,* he whimpers. *Nem, nem, nem.* The Rec Center has also left a message, canceling his remaining classes and banning him from ever teaching at the center again. From the back of a cupboard, he retrieves a jug of Veezlaat he's kept for years, the jug he and Lola would've uncorked next had they not divorced, and drinks himself silly.

*

Meanwhile, growing up in the Saint Plato Orphanage, the unadopted Dennis takes to reading philosophy remainders donated to the place by Fedankgo's Used Books. He reads them again and again and unintentionally memorizes all of them and one day becomes an adjunct philosophy professor at the community college.

Over at the distillery, sensing that life has lacked substance ever since Father Prendergast met the Zamboni with his name on it, Lola Tcholar looks through the college's course catalog and lights upon Philosophy of Substance, which Dennis happens to be teaching. She enrolls. As the first class meeting ends, she sashays up to him and invites him to tour the Veezlaat facility. She seduces him there and soon leads him to the altar, the same altar as it happens where Father Prendergast's remains are encased.

Until recently, to supplement his adjunct's pay, an uninspired Dennis was whiling away his spare hours behind the counter at the Saint Plato Wawa. Now, in the college office he shares with countless other adjuncts and a large fluffy white cat, an inspired Dennis composes imaginative papers between classes on thinking and being. A number are published and respect for him grows in adjunct philosophy circles.

But respect is ever so trifling when one spends one's weekends in bed with one's bride. Or rolled off the bed onto the plush bedroom carpeting, or in the Jacuzzi or the shower, or on the dining room table, silverware and glassware askew. Especially if that bride happens to be Lola Tcholar and the honeymoon promises to be endless. They imbibe Veezlaat by the jug and enjoy the most outrageous sex. Dennis has never known anything like it. The woman is irresistible and insatiable and virtually erupts in sensual Hungarian screams, moans, and expletives whenever they do it. He makes no attempt to learn the language himself. The times the neighbors call the police aside, he experiences more delirious pleasure than any adjunct philosophy professor could ever possibly dream of.

That marriage comes to an unexpected end at an international convention of adjunct philosophy professors in Paterson. During an afternoon break, sipping Veeslaat from his flask, Dennis spots Denise Dunedin, an adjunct from New Zealand, across the lobby. She waves. He hurries over to speak with her, some philosophical notion they'd left unresolved the day before. But halfway across the lobby he stumbles against a whirring floor fan. The flask makes contact with the fan. A slight clink. A few sparks. A faint thrum. Dennis is electrocuted. Adjunct philosophy professor Denise Dunedin detects a hint of something burnt in the air.

Lola is hanging out in the Saint Plato Diner, sipping Supremo spiked with Veezlaat, when the call comes on her cell phone notifying her about Dennis. He thinks no more and therefore isn't, she says aloud to no one in particular as she puts away her phone.

# PART III

# HERE AGAIN

# NINE

Outside, it's dark. Inside, Sebastian is perched on a Gideon Bible licking a paw. Dennis is ringing Molly to tell her they're well on their way home.

Hooray! Molly responds to the telling. The adventure concludes! No more distressing dreams for me—of you driving from Pizza Hut to Pizza Hut relentlessly searching for Miss Elusivity. Where are you now?

In Ohio for the night. And Sebastian says, Praise the Lord! But I'm wondering, is it hot there?

Er, no. It's December, Dennis. This is New Jersey. Why would it be hot here?

Uh. It's hot in Ohio. Way above normal. It's been hot everywhere.

Not in good old normal New Jersey! It's cold, just like it should be this time of year. The new waitress? Denise? She'd be half frozen except for the warm clothes I've been loaning her. I never told you, she came here from Maui.

*Maui?* She came to Saint Plato from *Maui?* Why?

Her roots are here, that's why. That's what the fortune cookie she found on Ho'okipa Beach said. And that she'd travel here for the details. And that her harpoon would prove handy. But she'd have a cow getting them to let her on the plane with it.

Are you being silly, Molly?

Well, sorta a little bit about the cow.

You're sorta sleeping with her a little bit too, I bet.

Nah. She's staying at your house with me but she's insufferably straight. Just like you. Besides, I'm a married woman.

There's giggling in the background.

Uh-huh, Dennis says.

But really, she did bring her harpoon. She's a champion harpoonist.

Sure. Just like Sally what's-her-name was a champion

111

chess player. Surely you make that up.

Me? Molly says. Make that up? Never! Sally what's-her-name's beside the point.

She was the best chess player in Saint Plato, Dennis says.

For all the good it did her. Hey! Valentine Funk? Gracious's kid?

Er, yeah.

Speaking of making things up, that contest for making up the best story about how Saint Plato got its name? Valentine won. Silas Punterponk was the judge. He says the story is in a league of its own. Apparently it has the town named after a canonized Greek mercenary. I haven't read it. I've been too busy not sleeping with Denise.

There's a squeal in the background and the call's dropped.

Molly calls back: Seriously, Dennis, Denise wants to save herself for you.

Another squeal.

Uh-huh.

We'll have a big party when you get here. A day or two yet? You're in Ohio?

Yeah. The same Happy Inn we stayed at in Zanesville last month going the other way. You know, Zane Grey's from Zanesville, but the town's not named after him. It's named after Colonel Ebenezer Zane.

Gee whiz, Molly teases. Not a canonized Greek mercenary.

Uh, no. Zane Grey was named after him too. The colonel was an ancestor of his from West Virginia except it wasn't West Virginia then. And he built the first major path in Ohio, right along where we were driving today.

The first *major path?* Like he was only a major when he built it? Not yet a colonel?

My source didn't say.

Your *source?*

Some guy in the hot tub here last time.

You were in a hot tub with a *guy?*

And Sebastian. The guy was a salesman from Dayton, married with children.

That's what they all say.

Uh, anyway, I wanted to tell the original Denise about Colonel Zane and Zanesville when I phoned her that night. But she didn't have time to listen.

The poor woman! Molly says. Missing out on such fascinating stuff!

Um. Ask me why she didn't have time to listen.

Okay, why?

Because she was giving Tuffy a philosophy quiz. Tuffy, her cat.

Hmmm. Did Tuffy pass?

She should have. She studied two nights straight for it.

Hurry home, Dennis. It's definitely not normal out there.

# TEN

Hey, Sebastian! They're in the Cruiser heading east after breakfast at the Zanesville Happy Inn. You wanna hear about Sally what's-her-name? She had a cat named Kasparov.

*Irrrph.*

So what's with this Sally what's-her-name? the waitress Denise also asks Molly when they're up and about in the morning.

You mean, what *was* with her, Molly says. She was gunned down at Saint Plato's last ever chess championship. Right after she choked the life out of that cheating little snot, Chester Fedankgo.

You couldn't blame her, Dennis tells Sebastian. Chester had cheated his way to the championship again, beating her for the seventh year in a row. Molly might've strangled him if Sally hadn't.

\*

Sally never existed. Neither did Chester. There was no *there*. Saint Plato has never had a chess championship.

Molly and Dennis made up Sally and Chester and the championship—and a lot more—after two unruly players in a corner booth at the diner, the only booth where chess was played and then only occasionally, descended into an unholy scrum, flinging insults and their chess pieces at each other, and the dregs of their borscht specials, and their bowls and spoons.

Imbeciles! Molly proclaimed, wiping up borscht. After which she hand-printed a sign and taped it to the door: *NO CHESS! EVER AGAIN!*

Dennis retrieved a king, a bishop, and some pawns that had skittered his way and tossed them into the trash.

Made-up Sally was a secretary at Saint Plato Central High, Dennis tells Sebastian and Molly tells Denise. She'd graduated from *there*, spent half her life *there*. Thirty-something and single, she'd dated the swimming coach on and off until his disgraceful attempt to get her to skinny-dip in the high school pool.

Chess and her cat Kasparov were what mattered to her. Year after year she'd been runner-up to Chester Fedankgo in the championships. Year after year Chester cheated. Each year, she'd swear she'd kill him. She knew that if she did, she'd be wasted by his notorious half-uncles who always attended the championships. So she made a will.

Everyone knew Chester Fedankgo was a snot. Everyone knew he cheated.

So what? his mother would say.

Prove it! his father would say.

Prove it! is also what his father challenged the police to do when they accused him of harboring his half-brothers, the late Chester's half-uncles. He wasn't harboring anyone. The monks at Our Lady of Saint Plato Abbey were doing the harboring. The half-uncles are still at the abbey, disguised as their harborers. They insist they didn't do it, that they were set up, that it was the judge at the championship who snuffed Sally with his starter pistol that wasn't a starter pistol, that the judge was a homicidal maniac in a witness protection program. He'd ratted on the Mahwah mob.

*

Isn't that a bit far-fetched? Dennis interjected back when he and Molly were making it up.

Well, call it the Metuchen mob then, Molly said.

Um, that's not what I meant.

I know that's not what you meant.

Oh.

Speaking of starter pistols that aren't starter pistols, Mrs. Fedankgo keeps one behind the bar at Fedankgo's Saloon. She and Dennis's Mirabelle used to hang out at demolition derbies at Fedankgo Speedway and fire the pistol into the air. Mirabelle once drove a battered pickup truck in a demolition derby for pickups there. She never let on where she got battered truck.

When not cleaning her pistol, Mrs. Fedankgo is said to water down the Our Lady of Saint Plato Pale Ale on tap at the saloon. The diner's Greek dishwasher once complained that his draft pale ale tasted weak.

WEAK? I'll give you weak! Mrs. Fedankgo shouted, filling a pitcher. This one's on the house! She dumped most of it on his head, then sloshed the rest over his beard. Dennis drank only bottled pale ale there.

*

Made-up Sally bequeathed her runner-up trophies to the high school. *Space can be made for them,* she suggested in her will, *by getting rid of all the stupid stuffed hedgehogs in the display case in the main lobby.* The stuffed hedgehogs were the school's mascots that had died.

The first time Sally lost to Chester Fedankgo, at the finals of the first championship, Chester was five years old and the antithesis of a chess prodigy. He remained antithetical to the end. His lack of ethical principles overcame his lack of skill.

Sally, on the other hand, was good. Very good. And she knew it. I'm the best chess player in Saint Plato, she'd say.

She might never have played, ever, and might still be alive, in a never-having-existed sort of way, if it hadn't been for the make-believe Dennis. He was Sally's boyfriend in high school and tried to get her to play strip chess with him before she knew anything about the game. But Sally was no fool—she joined the school's chess club first to learn all she could. Dennis eschewed clubs.

Whoa! the real Dennis said. You're make-believing me into a loathsome chess player and a teenage lech *and* the cause of Sally's death?

Relax, Molly said. You never had a girlfriend in high school. I'm giving you one. Enjoy the made-up moment.

*

Sally quickly mastered the fundamentals, then began improvising brilliantly. In her first real game she checkmated Sergey Sikorsky, the club's president, before you could say *Sergey Sikorsky*. He was inconsolable and had to be institutionalized.

She remembered him in her will. *I bequeath to Sergey Sikorsky my rare set of bamboo chess pieces, hand-carved by Polynesian outrigger paddlers if you want to believe that malarkey. I regret that Sergey is still institutionalized and allowed to play chess only with himself.*

After Sergey lost it, that very same night Sally set up a board and invited Dennis over to play. Her parents had gone out. He tore to her house, but it wasn't long before he tore back out, scrambling through a window in only his underpants, all but checkmated. Sally's parents had gotten home early. She hadn't had to unbutton even one button.

*Because of his vow of poverty, I can only bequeath an apology to Dennis. He didn't stand a chance of beating me. It's just as well he gave up the game after that. But is it weird or what? Him a monk now at Our Lady of Saint Plato Abbey?*

*

That was Dennis's idea, himself becoming a monk. Not because he was religious. Which he wasn't.

I'll rub out a few monks and become abbot, he said.

Or you could sleep your way to the top, Molly giggled.

Molly! I couldn't do that. I'm not of that persuasion, you know.

No, Molly laughed, you're not! You're a moral basket case is what you are. Not to mention a make-believe disappointment.

*

Sally brought Kasparov to the finals of the first championship, in the high school gym. Chester was late and brought several cushions. Kasparov hissed at him as he piled the cushions onto his chair so he could reach the board like a normal person. Settled, he drew white, moved first, and started humming. Sally complained.

He's only five, the judge said. Let him hum.

Then Chester started cheating. The worst was when he moved his rook diagonally, jumped a pawn, and captured Sally's queen, putting her king in check. You can't do that! she shouted. He shrugged and punched the clock.

Judge! she called out. He can't do that!

He's only five, the judge shrugged.

Chester stuck out his tongue at Sally. Kasparov hissed again. This is fair? Sally shouted and got up and went after Chester. She got hold of him for a moment, but he was all slimy and he screamed and squirmed away from her and ran.

She lost.

The next week Mihal came into the school office. Mihal was the new exchange student from Romania and he was upset. Sally'd heard he'd joined the chess club. He was upset because his host family had taken to playing Romanian operas whenever he was doing his homework.

They're just trying to make you feel at home, Sally told him, to show solidarity with Romania.

Ha, he said. They not know about Romania any hardly fuck-all.

Mihal had that irresistible English-as-a-second-language way of expressing himself. And he was awfully cute. She invited him to do his homework at her house. She told him Kasparov's purring would be the loudest sound in the house.

Until, she told herself, *she* started purring. It's not like I'm a teacher or anything, Sally reasoned. It's nothing like *those* kinds of stories you hear about. I'm just a secretary.

Mihal said he liked cats. He began sneaking out of the opera house and across town to Sally's back door. She waited until the second time he was there before bringing out the chessboard, let him capture the first piece, and unbuttoned her shirt.

He blushed.

She went ahead and took off her shirt and quickly captured a pawn and said, Your turn.

Her second game ever of strip chess.

Mihal got little homework done that year and his grades weren't very good, but he went back to Romania a happy boy.

Sally bequeathed all her panties to him.

*No one ever treated my panties with such reverence. And Mihal gave me back my self-respect. I hope he can be found. Romania itself is hard to find.*

By the time Mihal went back to Romania a happy boy, Saint Plato's second annual chess championship was around the corner. Sally was looking forward to it. But it was as much a disaster for her as the first. She had the snot. She was three moves to mate. Which is when Chester threw up on the board.

He's only six, the judge said.

Sally hurled the board at the judge, splattering Chester's barf on him.

You'd think that over time Chester would've matured. Not so. At age seven—and Sally was winning handily again—he wet his pants, then knocked over his bottle of Mountain Dew to divert attention. His pants and the board got soaked. In the commotion, he slid a couple of his chess pieces through the slop to more advantageous positions.

At eight, he pulled his toy bot out from underneath his shirt and let it loose on the board, upsetting her pieces that had been close to victory.

At nine, sorely outplayed, he requested a bathroom break and eluded his escort long enough to turn on a cell phone he'd swiped and call in a bomb scare for the gym. Sally bequeathed her furniture-grade chessboard with oak-stained squares to the Saint Plato Volunteer Bomb Squad.

*The board was made for me in the high school shop by a secret admirer who later revealed himself and proposed to me in a letter from Iraq. It was so sweet. Before I could respond he was killed by an acronym. I would have gone to Iraq. I would have married him there. I would have protected him from IEDs.*

*

How could she have protected him? Dennis asked.

She would've found a way, Molly said. Maybe made him a magic cloak. Or gotten the idiots that started the war to call it off.

Making a magic cloak would've been easier, Dennis said.

*

At ten, Chester opened innocuously with P-K4 and started staring at Sally's breasts. It must've been the particular sweater she was wearing. He kept it up the whole game. It was one of the worst games she ever played. Still she almost forced a draw. She whispered to him afterward that his weenie would fall off into the toilet the next time he peed.

Did you hear what she said? Did you hear what she said? he stammered in duplicate to those nearby.

Sally walked silently away, smug in her belated cool.

Leading up to the seventh annual championship, she noted that in a couple of years Chester would be in high school—if he lived that long. As a secretary at the high school, she'd have opportunities to alter his records and irrevocably besmirch his already perverse existence. She could change all his grades to F and make up symptoms of contagious diseases on his school nurse forms and forge a doctor's letter mandating mortifying restrictions on him and contrive affidavits of psychopathic tendencies that would make him unfit to join the chess club.

Yet she believed such measures wouldn't be necessary.

120

She was going to walk away as champion this time. Or kill the snot.

*

Kasparov helped her prepare. Once when he was tenderly moving pieces around with his paw he solved an end-game problem she'd been working on.

Kindly old Mr. Jeepers from across the street helped too. He was blind, but he studied the game using books on tape and felt his way around the board. Kasparov liked to curl up on his lap. Sometimes Mr. Jeepers would nod off and his head would flop down on the board, scattering the pieces. Which would startle him awake. Sally would joke that they should play strip chess together. Maybe that would keep you awake, she'd say. And I'd let you win.

Jeepers, he'd reply. Being blind, I'd see peeping-little of your breasts.

She bequeathed Kasparov to Mr. Jeepers, and all her bras. *They can be used like Braille,* she suggested in the will.

*

At that seventh and last championship the judge signaled that play was to begin by shooting his starter pistol that wasn't a starter pistol into the air. Bits of plaster crumbled down onto the crowd from the ceiling of the gym. One of Chester's half-uncles jumped out of his chair and stared straight up menacingly, a hand inside his jacket.

Time stood still. Or maybe went by very fast.

Chester had duplicates of the chess pieces in his pockets and each time Sally captured a piece he would sneak its duplicate onto the board.

Where'd that come from? Sally asked not too quietly, spotting a duplicate knight.

Wouldn't you like to know, Chester whispered.

He's using extra pieces, Sally complained to the judge.

He's only eleven, the judge said. Play on.

121

I will not, Sally said.

Then I declare Chester Fedankgo the champion, the judge said.

Fuck it, Sally said and climbed right over the table, grabbed the snot by the neck, and choked the life out of him.

Then bang bang bang bang bang. Most everyone believed the shots had come from where Chester's notorious half-uncles had been sitting. The half-uncles believed otherwise. But rather than argue the point, they charged out of the gym faster than a speeding rook.

\*

The Cruiser has now outrun the flat landscape that had stretched all the way from Indianapolis, the last of the flatness fading from the rearview mirror. Dennis and Sebastian have reached the rolling hills of eastern Ohio. It's still hot. The trees are bare, their leaves long fallen, but it's like a summer day.

Dennis has a plan, a surprise for Sebastian. He'll ignore the speed limit for once and drive recklessly through the upcoming sticking-up part of West Virginia, no slowing down, no chancing a fatal encounter with Beverly and her brood out on a shooting spree. Then into Pennsylvania and onward to Fallingwater, the Frank Lloyd Wright house on top of a waterfall. If it's still hot, Sebastian can go for a swim.

\*

Molly had a plan the night before. Dennis deserves a Denise, she knows. He's her best friend, they have history, she roots for him. But what harm to add a little Veezlaat to the new waitress's bedtime hot chocolate so that Molly can seduce her. Dennis will get over it. They shared Gabriela Gloriosa, sort of, didn't they?

\*

The make-believe Dennis had a plan as well. At some

point after Sally's wasted, he'd be in the middle of a sinful siesta with a make-believe Molly, his monk's robes and her consecrated-virgin's attire scattered on the floor of the Airstream trailer out by the pond at Our Lady of Saint Plato Abbey.

*

Um, the real Dennis said as the real Molly was making that up.

Look at it this way, Molly said. If you won't pretend to be gay, I'll pretend to be straight.

*

Brother Dennis wanted to marry Sister Molly, which was forbidden of course. But he'd find a way, maybe get a minister's certificate through one of those correspondence courses and marry himself and her himself.

He might not ever have set foot in the Airstream or anywhere at the abbey or any other where again had he not escaped a sticky situation at Fedankgo's Motel outside town, an escape that got him to the abbey to begin with, a situation more terrifying than sticky really. He was almost in the middle of his own dying.

He and his new flame, Joie, were just getting down to their underwear when Joie's husband burst into their room and tried to kill them both with his starter pistol that wasn't a starter pistol. Joie's husband was the chess judge.

For the second time in his made-up life, Dennis fled in panic in only his underpants. The gun jammed, but he was already running like hell all the way to the abbey where he was taken in. Joie ran like hell in a different direction, all the way to an out-of-the-way dive known as Hank's Hideaway, and spent the night disguised as a pole dancer. The motel's night manager considered forwarding the clothes they'd left strew about the room to the fake address in Wyoming that Dennis had put on the registration form. But the early crew of

123

undocumented Guatemalan housekeepers got first dibs.

Having come so close to his own dying, safe now, imbued with a profound appreciation of life, the fledgling Brother Dennis at first experienced much peace at the abbey—its buildings kneeling reverently in the meadows and woods a few miles from town, time measured by the gentle tolling of the bells, the unhurried processions of the monks into the chapel and out. Multiple gentle tollings and unhurried processions occurred before he began to understand that all was not as it appeared.

The monks' brains were jammed. Take that wizened illiterate lump, Brother Wally, coughing into a magazine he was holding upside down over at the periodicals table in the reading room, disrupting Dennis's concentration on an unauthorized biography of God that Fedankgo's Used Books had donated to the abbey.

You might try stuffing that magazine down your throat, an exasperated Dennis called out, in lieu of cough drops. Wally dropped the magazine and, keeping a worried eye on Dennis, retreated backwards out of the room, coughing in little chirps. Slouched in a chair in a corner, one of the half-uncles set aside the Beretta he'd been cleaning and gave Dennis a thumbs-up.

Francine, the guesthouse cook, had been blabbing that Wally was a pervert. Abbot Adam told her that, told her he'd watched Wally fondling the abbey's statue of Our Lady of Saint Plato. Francine was being humped by Adam and he told her stuff he shouldn't have. He did keep to himself that he wanted to make a video of Wally fondling the statue. But he didn't know how to make a video.

Not only were the monks' brains jammed, Dennis realized, but most of them were lunatics. Wally was loony, of course. And Adam. And Brother Peter, the resident fanatic, pacing furiously back and forth everywhere, swinging his rosary beads menacingly, praying for the Inqusition to be restored. And Brother Barfolo who never washed. He'd make Dennis gag.

A dark side of Dennis emerged. Maybe the half-uncle would give him Beretta lessons.

Brother Aquinox he liked, sort of—even if he was a prissy.

He washed every day and usually was rational. He was the abbey's spokesmonk after the communion bread hit the fan, his affected voice on the evening news calling several mysterious deaths at the abbey *an unfortunate accumulation of coincidental tragedies.*

*

Imagine us actually watching that on the *News at 6,* the real Dennis said to Molly.

Yeah, Molly replied. And what a catch that make-believe runt would be for a fag I know.

I suppose Aquinox would have to be gay.

Incalculably so. Your make-believe self exhausts the abbey's quota of straight monks.

What about Abbot Adam?

Francine's a transsexual.

Are you sure?

Hey, would I make something like that up?

*

*Coincidental tragedies* was one way of looking at the body count. Peter gone missing, parts of him turning up in the woods, Barf in a terminal coma, Wally dead in the pond. No one suspected foul play.

It began with Peter and no Beretta was needed. Dennis was in the laundry room doing the guesthouse sheets. He'd been demoted to abbey launderer after Adam found out he'd been urging customers in the gift shop to pray for anarchy. It was a joke, Dennis insisted. What did Adam know? He probably couldn't even spell *anarchy.* The word around the cloister was that he read Bible comics.

Anyway, Peter. He was looking for trouble, swaggering into the laundry room, coming up behind Dennis, clearing his throat in that disgusting way he'd perfected, sticking his pointy nose into another biography Dennis was reading, this one of an unauthorized God.

125

Dennis set the book down and went over to the dryer to check on the sheets. This trash you read, Peter said in his obnoxious, superior tone, picking up the book, raising his voice now, is written by *heretics*. He flung the book across the room.

Your screws are too tight, Dennis said.

My screws are just right, Peter said. He stomped up to him and peered into his face.

Dennis took a swipe at his pointy nose. Just a little swipe really, just to scare him, and he meant for it to miss. But it didn't. And damned if Peter didn't utter one of his disgusting sounds, drop his rosary, gape for a few seconds at a spot just above Dennis's head, and collapse onto the floor.

Blood trickled from his nose. He didn't seem to be breathing.

The sheets were still moist, so Dennis restarted the dryer and stepped over Peter and went and fixed himself a bowl of popcorn in the refectory. He munched the popcorn and guzzled a bottle of Our Lady of Saint Plato Pale Ale and tried to figure how he could explain what had happened.

Best not to, he concluded. He finished munching and guzzling just in time for Compline which was uplifting without Peter's maniacal, intrusive off-key chanting. Rather, the soft lilt of Sister Molly's voice washed over him from the pews where she sat, a stray fluffy white kitten she called Holy Spook on her lap. It sounded like a pop ballad she was singing though. The monks were chanting psalms.

Molly showed up at the abbey not long after Dennis. She looked just like Joie. She told him she was Joie's twin and made it clear the *consecrated virgin* nonsense was nonsense, a category Abbot Adam put her in so she could live on the property. She'd murmured to Adam that she'd been a swinger but now wanted to atone. And Adam, envisioning he wasn't sure what, maybe that she could make videos, let her move into the Airstream out by the pond. It had been Brother Zeke's hermitage before he abandoned it for a treehouse from where he could watch everything.

Brother Dennis fell for Sister Molly the first time he saw her. Her lovely large chocolate eyes, just like Joie's, her knowing smile, her quiet sensuality. He volunteered to mow the grass around the pond and, wouldn't you know, the tractor stalled in front of the Airstream. What was he to do but go up and knock on the door and ask her to run away with him to Xanadu? She laughed and brought out two bottles of pale ale she'd grabbed that morning from the abbey brewery's loading dock. They sat on the Airstream's steps and drank the ale and played with Holy Spook and talked of remaking the universe. Zeke watched from the treehouse.

The next mowing, the tractor stalled again and they were suddenly in each other's arms. Dennis wasn't quite sure how it happened.

*

Well actually, the real Dennis said, he was sure, but he wasn't telling.

Buttons were unbuttoned, Molly said, and Sister Molly called out, Jesus, Molly, and Dennis!

Hmmm. And what happened to Joie, do you think?

Joie pole-danced her way to California and is now in film.

You have lovely large chocolate eyes yourself, you know.

Don't get fresh, Dennis.

*

Picture Brother Dennis creeping back to the laundry room after everyone else but Peter had gone to bed, the drops of holy water from the abbot's sprinkler evaporated from their receding hairlines. Peter lay crumpled on the floor just as he'd been left, still not breathing. Dennis grabbed his ankles and dragged him out of the room, out of the building, and into the woods, across the uneven, gnarled ground and decaying leaves until his arms hurt. From above, in the dark, Zeke could just make out Dennis kicking up some leaves around what had been Peter, then hurrying back, brushing past rough tree trunks and brittle low limbs, exhilarated.

Adam announced at lunch the next day that Peter was

missing. Later, some gnawed-on bones were found, and half a rosary. A hungry bear? Perhaps an extended family of hungry bears escaped from a fairy tale. The bones and the half rosary were put in a defective Our Lady of Saint Plato tote bag from the gift shop and buried in the abbey's little cemetery.

At the burial, Barfolo stood next to Dennis. His smell was sickening. First chance Dennis had, he crushed a scoopful of unlabeled pills from the dispensary and mixed them into Barf's fiber supplement. Barf smelled so bad when the paramedics arrived that they thought he was already dead. That would take a few days.

Then Wally met his end. That was Molly's doing. The pervert had tried to fondle her down by the pond. She'd been in a yoga stance and Wally must have thought she was a statue. He had only a moment yet to live and realize his mistake. Molly shoved him into the pond and left him for dead, which he was, his head colliding with a rock on his way in. Zeke, woken by the splash, noted Wally floating in peace and resumed his nap.

Molly told Dennis but otherwise kept what happened to herself, and Wally's demise devolved into an unwitnessed anomaly. Adam couldn't praise him enough at the funeral. He'd been contemplating making a video of him, he said, highlighting his exemplary habits. Privately, he was recalling how excited he'd felt watching Wally fondle the statue of Our Lady of Saint Plato. And how scorched he was going to feel in hell. Adam heard his own confession, gave himself a hundred Holy Wallys to say for penance, and stipulated there'd be no absolution until he relinquished Francine.

God is issuing ultramaydooms, he told her in the guesthouse kitchen as she was rinsing a carving knife. I must uncouple myself from thee.

Adam's blood-drenched remains were found crumpled on the guesthouse kitchen floor, slashed twenty-nine times. Francine was rumored to be on her way to Ecuador.

Just days earlier the good Brother Aquinox had appeared on the news, but now a certain Major Brother Spike appeared at the abbey, arriving on a vaporetto by way of the creek.

128

A vaporetto? Dennis asked. On Saint Plato Creek?

Sure, Molly said. From Holy Headwaters.

*

Major Brother Spike put himself in charge and proclaimed a news blackout. Which was very bad news for *29 Minutes.* Twenty-nine slashes! It would've been the program's signature story.

Nor, Spike decreed, were the events to be discussed among the monks. Aquinox kept his mouth shut and took to meditating down by the pond on unfortunate accumulations of coincidental tragedies. At siesta time on his first day of meditation and again on his second he beheld Brother Dennis stealthing toward Sister Molly's trailer. On the third day he stopped meditating and followed, creeping slowly after him toward the Airstream. By the time he was close enough to hear, Dennis and Molly were combining their orgasms. Aquinox stood still and listened, then crept closer as the sounds reached a crescendo. And crept closer yet, on up to the window, and peered in.

Orgasmed out, Molly opened her eyes, blinked once, and realized what she was looking at out the window was Aquinox looking in. She made a very different sort of sound. Aquinox ran. Dennis caught him before he got very far.

Let go of me, Brother! Aquinox commanded feebly. You were doing things to Sister Molly and, and, and—in an oddly hushed tone—you don't have any clothes on. Which was true. Dennis had rushed out after him that way. He blushed.

I'm conscience-bound, Aquinox continued breathlessly, to report your unconscionability.

Unconscionability?

It would be his last word.

Or second last.

Oh, you shouldn't report my anything, Dennis replied,

half amused, still blushing, shaking him gently, adding, Unconscionability is what makes the world go round. Aquinox flopped this way and that and was trying to say something more:

Unless—

That's what it sounded like, several times over:

Unless—

Unless—

But then he started burbling and a look of astonishment came over his face and he collapsed.

A look of astonishment came over Dennis's face, too. After Peter, the odds against something similar happening again were astronomical. Dennis pondered this. Not to mention that, really, what sort of a pin-headed name was *Aquinox?* He'd never thought to ask him when he was alive.

Holy Spook pouncing on her untied shoelaces the whole way, Sister Molly hustled out with Dennis's clothes. She checked for Aquinox's pulse, confirmed that he was no longer Aquinox, and said, Fuck.

Zeke climbed down from his treehouse with a plan. The late Brother Aquinox was found under the brewery's loading dock, a peaceful look on his face, a few dozen empty bottles of pale ale scattered about. The abbey hasn't been the same without him. And whenever Dennis cuts through the cemetery on his way to a siesta with Molly, passing Aquinox's little white cross there next to Barf's, he's overcome with disbelief.

They were lovers, you know, Zeke whispered to Dennis at the funeral.

They?

Aquinox and Barfolo.

But—

Zeke just looked at him and smiled and nodded.

*

But, Dennis said to Molly, if Aquinox had been doing it with Barfolo, why would it matter to him about Brother Dennis and Sister Molly?

130

Jealousy, Molly said. Aquinox had it in mind to blackmail you. He never got the whole sentence out. He would report us *unless* you would—you know—have sex with *him*.

*

Major Brother Spike put himself on tranquilizers and decreed that the monks still living could either kill each other off or elect a new abbot, it was all the same to him, he'd had it, he'd be out of there on the next vaporetto back to Holy Headwaters.

Right after which Zeke approached Dennis, told him he'd been watching him all along and he liked his style, asked if he'd serve. Zeke controlled a number of votes, it seemed, and could arrange for the half-uncles to break a few arms if necessary.

*Abbot* Dennis! Dennis marveled. Who would've thought! I'll appoint Molly vice abbot. Ho boy!

*

Sebastian gets his first glimpse of the waterfall under the Frank Lloyd Wright house, lets out an ecstatic *irrrph!*

He and Dennis spent the night at a Happy Inn near Fallingwater and arrived with the first wave of tourists in the morning, everyone marveling at the hot weather, not noticing the cat trotting past the *No Fluffy White Pets Allowed* sign.

Not until he runs and leaps into the waterfall is Sebastian noticed.

Look, a flying squirrel! someone shouts.

Sebastian climbs out and gets another running start and leaps into the waterfall again. And again.

A whole troupe of *rare* fluffy white flying squirrels!

There are absolutely no rare fluffy white flying squirrels in this part of Pennsylvania, a guide tells the gathering crowd.

Now Sebastian is floating on his back in the pool under the waterfall.

Look, a rare fluffy white otter!

Cameras and cell phones photograph the fascinating wildlife at Fallingwater.

# ELEVEN

Philadelphia off to the right, Dennis and Sebastian minutes from crossing the Delaware, minutes from New Jersey.

It's *Anything Goes* time.

*Buongiorno,* Dennis.

Uh.

Can we still be friends? Would you like to be my honorary *paesano?*

Dennis's first impulse is to tell North Dakota Denise, No, they can't and he wouldn't, not after—

Instead, another *Uh.*

I'm calling from a cabana on the shores of the Great Salt Lake. Tuffy and I—

A cabana on the shores of the Great Salt Lake?

Sì. Just above the salt line. As I was about to say, Tuffy and I are preparing for our world concert tour. I'm training her to be my page turner. Imagine! From a sculpture park of outhouses to a Michelin-class pizza parlor to the Mormon Tabernacle and now—

The Mormon Tabernacle?

Sì. Tuffy and I were sharing a pepperoni and anchovies on a thin crust and I was humming a Gianni jingle between bites and a talent scout from the Choir rushed up, all excited, there were openings. He drove us to Utah in his red Rolls and I had a tryout and it would've been in the bag. Except I got caught painting my portrait on the Tabernacle. So I went and stood in the middle of Temple Square and started belting out jingles so everyone would understand what they'll be missing. And you know what? A bigtime promoter happened to be hawking Joseph Smith bobbleheads in the Square! He had a contract in my hand and was booking dates before I'd finished my encore! I'll be singing Giannis in concert all around the world! Aren't you happy for me?

Um.

The bridge over the Delaware is just ahead. Dennis slows

for the toll booths, sets the phone down next to Sebastian on the passenger seat.

The jingler continues: I can get you complimentary tickets. Some of the venues are standing room only already. Italia's completely sold out—Milano, Roma, Napoli. But there are good seats left in Bukhara. That's in Uzbekistan on the Silk Road. Would that be okay?

Silence.

Are you still there, Dennis?

More silence.

*Paesano?*

Rearranging himself, Sebastian accidentally knocks the phone off the passenger seat into his litter box. He peers down at the phone, then hops down into the litter box and covers it up.

Dennis and Sebastian are on the bridge now. Their future is in New Jersey's hands.

# TWELVE

Halfway across the state already, halfway across good old normal New Jersey, no hot weather in December this side of the Delaware, instead a hint of flurries in the air, refreshingly brisk snow.

Also in the air, overhead, a drone. It's been keeping pace with the Cruiser since the bridge. A *29 Minutes* drone, the lettering on it says. Sebastian might not mind, but Dennis does not want to be on *29 Minutes*. The intrusiveness, the exposure, the embarrassment. He wonders who could have tipped the program off about him. And how it managed to acquire a drone.

On the car radio, *Capriccio Italien,* the music an exclamation point to North Dakota Denise's Gianni jingles.

The drone drones on. *Capriccio Italien* plays on. Dennis has never cared for Tchaikovsky. As a kid he found a set of classical 45s on a curb on trash day, not something he was much interested in but there it was. Beethoven appealed to him, Bach, Chopin. But the Russian's music grated on him. He reaches to turn the radio off but sees Sebastian keeping time with the composition. Little twitches with his tail, little kneadings with his paws. Or is Dennis misinterpreting? No, the twitches and kneadings are in time with the beat, definitely. Well, if Sebastian likes Tchaikovsky—

And they're almost back now, they're almost back to Saint Plato, the only place Dennis has ever known as home. There's comfort in that. And of knowing the waitress Denise is saving herself for him. Ha! Molly was joking, of course. They've probably done it, the two of them, knowing Molly.

Not only does Dennis let Tchaikovsky be, he even starts *tra-la-la*-ing and *da-de-da*-ing to the music. Sebastian stops twitching and kneading and stares at him.

Dennis imagines waltzing the waitress Denise around the diner to *Capriccio Italien,* waltzing her out the diner door, down Main Street and back, screw the drone. If *Capriccio Italien* can be waltzed to. It doesn't matter, they'll waltz to it anyway, even if he's never waltzed since grade school. With Molly then, a dance lesson for sixth graders instead of gym that day. Even if he can't remember how, today he'll waltz and waltz and waltz with the waitress Denise. And with Molly too. And Sebastian. He'll hold Sebastian in his arms and waltz and waltz.

*Capriccio Italien* ends.

An announcer comes on. The station is in the middle of a fund drive, broadcasting live from the diner. For a contribution of however much, you get a CD of Tchaikovsky as a thank-you gift. For another however much, a copy of Silas Punterponk's memoirs—if he ever finishes writing them.

Mr. Punterponk will read an excerpt now from a finished chapter. When you're ready, Silas.

*

Thank you. Silas clears his throat. Um, yes. An excerpt. This is from Chapter 39. Or, um, 36. I haven't written 39 yet. He clears his throat again. Yes. Here we go. It was a hot and humid afternoon. I'd found Denise, that was her name, the name I'd given her.

Huh? Dennis says out loud in the car.

She'd eluded me once. But now I'd found her. She was subletting a second-floor walk-up on Main Street, just down the block from the diner. The air-conditioning wasn't working, it hadn't been since she moved in, parts of her T-shirt were soaked with sweat. She looked more luscious than ever in a lugubrious sort of way.

More luscious than ever in a lugubrious sort of way? Dennis says, out loud again.

*Irrrph.*

Silas reads on: I'd been searching for her ever since I'd caught a glimpse of her shoplifting deodorant from the Dollar Store. Shoplifting was out of character though, and how could she still be around anyway? Yet there she was, or a fleeting bit of her, despite having been deleted from the novel I was writing.

Having been deleted from the novel he was writing?

Dennis says.

*Irrrph-iphrrph.*

Irrrph-iphrrph? Dennis approximates.

It was never finished, Silas continues. So you might expect she would have the last laugh. All my novels have never been finished. My novellas too. And my short stories. But no need to dwell on that.

When I knocked on Denise's door, she didn't answer at first. I had to knock again and when she finally opened the door, I introduced myself as a life insurance salesman. She didn't recognize me.

I hadn't wanted to be seen like this, she said. It's not the freaking heat. Or the freaking humidity. Oh, no. It's the freaking depression. I need to score some whoopee pills. I mean, one day I'm gonna live happily forever and the next day—

She slid a finger across her throat.

I told her I was sorry. I had no whoopee pills, only life insurance applications.

Yeah, well, *c'est la* freaking *vie,* she said. But it's not so simple. I've no past, no future. Technically no present. Life insurance wouldn't make sense, would it? And yet I'm stuck here.

I asked why she couldn't just leave.

Where would I go? she replied. Not back to wherever it was the freaking author had me come from. Quebec? They wouldn't let me across the border. With my past wiped out, I'm no longer a Canadian citizen. I'm not an American citizen either. I'm a bilingual woman without a country.

I'd never thought of that. And I hadn't the heart to tell her I'd replaced her in the novel with a hot-blooded señorita from Sonora. Also bilingual come to think of it.

Come to think of it? Dennis mumbles.

Sebastian has dozed off.

Silas: Denise lit a Gitane for herself, didn't offer me one. She blew out a stream of smoke and said, The guy downstairs in the French café, he brought these back from Montreal. I think he likes me. But he's married.

And it wouldn't be like you to mess around with a married

man, I said. But how come you're smoking? You never used to smoke.

She gave me an odd look and asked, How the freak would you know? and took a long drag on her Gitane. I was blowing my cover, you see. I'd already blown it. She started shouting at me. Stuff like *NOM DE DIEU!* and YOU'RE the FREAKING AUTHOR! AREN'T YOU? She took a quick drag and violently stubbed out her cigarette and wailed, Why did you come here?

I fumbled for the right words. I'm, well, I was hoping maybe, uh, you are looking more luscious than ever, Denise, in a lugubrious sort of way. That's what I said. And then I said, Let us go then, you and I, to a movie tonight at the Bijou. Or I'll pick up some oysters and we could stay in. *I'm* not married.

She glared at me and screamed, GET OUT! GET OUT!

I edged toward the door. She followed, pushed me hard. Okay, I said. She pushed again. Okay! I was at the top of the stairs. She shoved me down them.

I came to in the hospital, in Saint Plato General. Freddy Gonzalez-Schmidt was on duty in the ER and he listened with his stethoscope and told me I might never write again.

Fooled him all right. I was back at my vintage Royal splickety-lit, pecking out a flash fiction about Denise, short enough to finish on the spot. And back to her place to show it to her, hoping she'd be forgiving. But she was gone, the walk-up was empty.

*

Without comment, the radio station begins the *1812 Overture.*

Dennis fantasizes looking for Silas's Denise himself. He'd ask about her in the French café but the owner would say he knows of no Denise. And no one's ever lived upstairs, it's a storeroom. And why would he go to Montreal? He's not French. He's Norwegian. The First Bank of Saint Plato wouldn't approve a business loan for a Norwegian café.

Dennis would try the Dollar Store next. He'd hang out in the deodorant aisle until the clerk got suspicious. He'd want

138

to say, It's okay, I'm a librarian. Or used to be. But he'd feel foolish and leave.

*

That familiar sign:
*Welcome to Saint Plato, New Jersey*
*A Designated Hedgehog Sanctuary*
The Cruiser's soon passing the Bijou. *Only Lovers Left Alive.* Tilda Swinton. She was so sexy in *Michael Clayton.* Evil but sexy. Dennis could invite the waitress Denise to see the new film with him. He parks in front of the diner. Overhead, the drone drones in place. He gathers up Sebastian, hurries inside. Molly Minnelli drops everything, rushes over, hugs them both.

There's a *29 Minutes* drone after me, Dennis says.

It's been bugging everyone, Molly says. Ignore it.

I don't want to be on the program.

You won't. Steps are being taken. Come sit in a booth, calm down. Sebastian, sweetheart, how about the bouillabaisse special? Your Dennis isn't relaxed enough to eat.

*Irrrph-iphrrph!*

Irrrph-iphrrph indeed! Molly's off to the kitchen. And back quickly with a bowl of bouillabaisse. The cat digs in.

The classical station was broadcasting from here, Molly says. Silas read from his memoirs.

Yeah, Dennis says. We were listening in the car. What he read was sorta absurd.

Silas is sorta absurd. Molly pours him a cup of decaffeinated Supremo. Life is sorta absurd.

Skoal, Dennis says, barely lifting the cup. He looks around. Is Denise here?

She's out taking care of some business. The drone's been after her too.

She's had an online dating disaster?

Not that I know of. Silas says it has to do with her roots, the drone being after her. He seems to know something. But it's like he's angling for a weekend in the sack with her before he'll tell. Denise says he'd better watch it or she'll ram her

139

harpoon up his. How about I put on some Tchaikovsky? The radio station left a CD.

\*

Dennis is trying to waltz with a giggling Molly to *Capriccio Italien*. Molly, however, is trying to mambo, a Maui mambo Denise has been showing her.

What does Denise look like anyway? Dennis asks.

Oh, I don't know. Sexy. Maybe like Ellen Barkin in *The Big Easy*. We saw it together. Remember?

Yeah. We both liked Ellen Barkin.

Mmmm. I would've done a threesome.

Molly!

You don't believe me?

I don't think so. But you two have done it, haven't you? You and Denise?

Before she can answer, there's an explosion somewhere outside. They look at each other and half waltz, half mambo, half run out the door to investigate. Sebastian stays put, licking up invisible remnants of his bouillabaisse from the bowl.

The drone is gone. A column of smoke is rising in the distance.

Hmmm, Molly says.

What? Dennis asks.

I think it's the drone. I think it crashed. Denise was going to try to shoot it down with her harpoon.

You can't be serious.

Yes I can.

The diner's phone starts ringing. That's probably her, Molly says. She said she'd call and let me know how it went.

Back inside, Molly picks up the phone. It is Denise. Molly puts the phone on speaker.

I shot it down! Denise exclaims. I harpooned the drone! It was like a giant avocado pit sputtering across the sky, a giant toothpick sticking out of it. And me dangling from the rope that dangled from the harpoon. Wheeeee! I'm at the abbey. That's where it crashed. A bunch of monks came running out of the chapel with their guns drawn. They're shooting at a tree now, shooting down chestnuts to roast over the flames.

Did you hear that, Dennis? Molly says. The drone's in flames!

Denny and Sebastian have arrived? Denise asks, excited.

They have, Molly says. We party tonight! Say hello to Dennis.

Hi, Denny.

Denny? No one's ever called him Denny. You really shot down the drone?

Sure. I'm a champion harpoonist, Denny. Would you like me to harpoon a pineapple off the top of your head?

Er, no.

Would you like to get in my pants?

No! I mean, I didn't mean that, it's just—

Didn't Molly tell you I'm easy, Denny?

Uh, why do you keep calling me Denny?

It's cute.

I've always been called Dennis.

*Dennis* isn't cute. Hey! Tonight we meet! Mmmmm.

*

You never said whether you and Denise have done it, Dennis reminds Molly.

Molly laughs. I never did, did I? You and Sebastian, go home now, unpack, rest up for your party!

*

It was hackers in Cambodia, Silas Punterponk is saying. He's just sat down next to Dennis on a love seat from Ikea. The party's in full swing. Dennis is taking a breather, Sebastian on his lap, tail twitching to an old Joni Mitchell tune. Molly sometimes fantasizes she's having an extramarital affair with Joni Mitchell. There's no sign of the waitress Denise.

In Cambodia? Dennis says to Silas. Hackers.

Whatever they're called, Silas says. The CIA's been

141

outsourcing its eavesdropping. A lot of what the Cambodians were picking up was useless. Like your phone conversations with that Denise from North Dakota.

You know about those?

Well, yeah. When Langley rejected them, the Cambodians sold them to *29 Minutes*. The program aired a preview.

Jesus. And the drone? How did it acquire a drone?

It was military surplus. Definitely military surplus.

*

Molly quiets the crowd, a good-sized crowd crowded into Dennis's house to welcome him home. Gracious Funk is there. She danced with him and kept her shirt on. Valentine is there too, Gracious's kid, and Leelagh Bobowicz and Ithy Funk and Mr. and Mrs. Edgarty, Funk's Funeral Home well represented. So too the college library and the Bijou. Lola Tcholar brought her latest squeeze, a computer nerd who's digitalizing the Veezlaat operations. Lulu from the Laundromat was seen heading upstairs with the Norwegian from the French café. Molly's LGBTQ gang is flitting about. She closed the diner for the night and, except for Denise, all its staff are partying. Now Molly has quieted the crowd, giving Valentine the floor to read his winning story on how Saint Plato got its name.

Scattered applause. Shouts of *Go get 'em, kid!* and *Up Saint Plato!*

*

*How Saint Plato Got Its Name,* Valentine begins. By Valentine Funk.

In 1776 the town was very small. It was called Creekburg. There were only a few log cabins and Fedankgo's Saloon and a bus stop in front of the saloon. My great-great-great-great-great-great-great-great-great-great-great-grandfather was the mayor. Christmas day he and George Washington were hanging out by the bus stop quaffing take-out flagons of Creekburg Pale Ale from the saloon and feeling no pain when a bus pulled up. A Greek-looking fellow got off.

Where the Zeus am I? the fellow said.

Creekburg, New Jersey, my great-great-great-great-great-great-great-great-great-great-great-grandfather said.

Oh shit! the fellow said. I got off at the wrong stop. But Creekburg! What a stupid name! You should change it. *Greek*burg would be better. *Saint Plato* would be best. That's my name. I'm a canonized Greek mercenary. I assist revolutionaries in crossing rivers.

Well, I'll be! George Washington said. Here, have a jolly quaff.

Hey thanks! Saint Plato grabbed George Washington's flagon, drained it, and said, Once I helped Napoleon cross the Seine. Then he grabbed my great-times-eleven-grandfather's flagon, drained it too, and went *Ahhhhh*. Now. Let's discuss your burg. You will be blessed by changing its name to mine. The burg will be blessed. *Saint Plato* has a nice ring to it, don't you think?

Um, my great-times-eleven-grandfather said. I don't know. How'd you get to be named Plato? Are you related to the philosopher?

Not at all, Saint Plato said. I'm a totally independent Plato. My name comes from a game of Scrabble.

What's Scrabble? George Washington asked.

It hasn't been invented yet, Saint Plato said. We Greeks are way ahead of the times. My mother was playing the game with the midwife while I was being born and the midwife had four letters left—lambda, pi, tau, and omega—and there was an unencumbered alpha on the board. She considered various combinations and finally spelled Plato.

That's not a word, my mother said as I uttered my first cry.

No, it's a boy, the midwife said.

Against all logic, the saint prevailed. Or just wore down my great-times-eleven-grandfather. As mayor, he proclaimed the name change then and there and the three of them retired to the saloon and toasted the new name through several more rounds.

Aren't you supposed to be crossing the Delaware tonight?

my great-times-eleven-grandfather asked George Washington during a lull in the toasts.

Yikes! George Washington said, looking at his watch. C'mon, Saint! Hurry! He ran to the door. We have to grab a bus over to the Pennsylvania side—where the boat is that we're gonna cross the Delaware with.

I charge by the hour, Saint Plato shouted, hustling after him. Plus expenses.

Martha'll write you a check, George Washington promised as they boarded the bus. By the way, where were you headed originally? And how'd you get to be a saint?

Originally? Saint Plato said. North Dakota. And I cannot tell a lie. I made the saint part up.

The end.

*

The applause is loud, sustained. Valentine bows. On the love seat, Sebastian has gone to sleep on Dennis's lap. Silas Punterponk applauds loudest and longest. That's my boy, he tells Dennis. That flair for words is in his genes.

You're Valentine's father? A touch of shrill incredibility in Dennis's voice.

It's in my memoirs, Silas says. Chapter 22.

You had an affair with Gracious? I don't want to believe you.

Ah, well, don't. But she flashed me one day at Trader Joe's and—

She flashed you—?

And speaking of fathers, I knew yours.

My father? You knew my father? What happened to him? Where is he? Is his name really FitzSweeney?

Your mother told you right. Sweeney FitzSweeney was his name. He swore me to secrecy. But I can divulge the whole story now with him departed.

Departed?

His ashes are scattered on a lake up in Saskatchewan.

Saskatchewan?

He was living the quiet life there in a ghost town called Old Wives. Well, people thought it was a ghost town. But he had his little harem.

A harem of old wives?

Not at all. The name's from an Indian legend. The average age in the harem was on the young side. They weren't wives either. Not his anyway.

Wasn't he from here?

I was just getting to that. He was a foundling. Found in a Veezlaat crate on the doorstep of the Saint Plato Orphanage. The name *Sweeney FitzSweeney* was embroidered on his diaper, but the orphanage thought that was too flamboyant a name for an orphan and called him Sam Smith and that stuck for years until he found out about the diaper. He went looking for his roots but no luck. Became a genealogist in the process and dabbled in that on and off. And he built a cabin out near the creek, Thoreau-like. You might say a ladies' Thoreau. One woman after another. He was the projectionist at the Bijou and often met them there. That's how your mother and he, uh, got together. Only for a few minutes or so on the floor of the projection booth but that's all it took.

On the floor of the projection booth? That's where I was—?

There'd been a power outage and he stayed up in the booth getting snockered—he kept a jug of Veezlaat up there—and it was very dark and all the patrons had gotten their money back and left except for your mother who was sitting alone in the dark in the balcony. She'd been unbearable, as usual, and her escort had excused himself, said he was going for popcorn, and never came back. And then the power went. Eventually she unbearabled herself into the projection booth and swigged some grog herself and next thing Sweeney FitzSweeney and Gladys Dunkle were—

I'm here because the popcorn guy didn't come back?

You could say that. When your father sobered and realized who he'd done it with, he packed a bag and held his breath. Your mother's reputation was abominable. She returned to the Bijou a few weeks later, a Bogart film was playing, and screeched at him. She was pregnant. She assured him his days were numbered.

Sebastian is wiggling the tip of his tail in his sleep. Dennis stares off into space, says, A wonder she didn't have an abortion.

Well, she considered it in fact. But it was illegal then and the one person here who would perform them under the table was a woman of color from Jamaica. Your mother wouldn't go to a woman of color.

Her bigotry saved me.

Precisely! When she returned to the Bijou that night, she'd already worked it out that she'd have you and hope for a girl, though she wasn't keen on girls either. Before she left she ripped apart the next Bogart reel, told Sweeney it was a preview of how he'd be ripped apart. She'd arrange it with the Fedankgos. He was out of there. Out of the Bijou. Out of Saint Plato. Out of New Jersey. The country. He used an alias for a while. Called himself Bogart in fact.

Bogart?

Bogart FitzBogart.

Dennis stares back into space. Sebastian tries to roll over in his sleep, slips, awakens, and rights himself, for balance attaching his front claws to Dennis's leg through his trousers.

Ow!

I ran into Fitz years later, Silas says, at a lecher convention in Saskatoon. Brought him up to date. He was amazed at your fortitude, how you were sticking it out here despite your mother, despite Mirabelle.

And despite no father, Dennis says.

Look at it this way. You were hardly his first child. Your mother was far from his first partner. For instance, he once had a tête-à-tête with Amelia Earhart.

Amelia Earhart?

She showed up in Saint Plato not long after she went missing in the Pacific and he welcomed her when she arrived, he was waiting for her, she had cabled him in advance. Her first night in town they had supper at the diner. She was famished and she finished off a whole roast chicken and extra orders of mashed potatoes and string beans and an entire banana cream pie. Your father ordered a BLT and a root beer but didn't finish either, he was so caught up listening to her telling him how she got rescued.

Amelia Earhart was having supper with my father in the diner? And telling him how she got rescued?

That's right. It was one of those Polynesian outrigger canoes that she got rescued with. Or in. Do you get rescued *with* a canoe or *in* it?

Uh, Dennis says. There's a reference work that might—

It's not important. She asked to be outriggered east and the outrigger crew didn't have anything better to do, they were just paddling back and forth between islands and carving bamboo chess pieces on layovers for the heck of it, so they agreed. She and that navigator fellow she was flying with wanted nothing to do with flying anymore and he got off at Acapulco and made a killing in sombreros. She directed the paddlers on down the Mexican coast and through the Panama Canal and up around Florida and north all the way to Saint Plato Creek.

Sebastian's gone back to sleep.

They'd had enough of paddling by then. They looked around for someone to paddle them home but no one wanted to. For a while they operated the South Pacific Theme Park and carved bamboo chess pieces for tourists. But Saint Plato didn't get many tourists and the park eventually shut down and the paddlers died out, never having gone home again and never revealing to anyone how they got here. Amelia Earhart made them promise. But you've got to be wondering why she wanted to be outriggered to Saint Plato in the first place.

Um—

She was looking for her roots, that's why. She believed there was FitzSweeney blood in her.

FitzSweeney blood? Why would she believe that?

I've no idea. But your father could sense it, that same renegade spirit that would envelope him watching a swashbuckler from the projection booth. She'd had the outriggerers paddle into Miami on the way and that's where she cabled him from, the same place she'd started out by plane on

147

her circumnavigation. So she completed the circumnavigation if you count the boat part. No one recognized her in Miami this time. She was wearing a Polynesian shirt and her hair had grown and gotten bleached in the sun.

But how did it happen she knew of my father? I don't see how—

Ah! She'd run across his name in a compendium of genealogists she'd been glancing at just before her plane went down. A miracle, she thought as the engine sputtered, a genealogist with the same name as my ancestors, maybe we're related.

In her cable she requested confidentiality, anonymity. What was Sweeney to do? Tell the world Amelia Earhart was alive and well and on her way to Saint Plato in an outrigger canoe? What would the world have thought of him if he'd done that? Of his trustworthiness? His loyalty? He kept it a secret.

Dennis absently runs a hand back and forth through Sebastian's fur. The cat starts purring in his sleep.

Silas: As the probable day of her arrival neared, Sweeney found someone to fill in for him at the Bijou and he camped out along the creek, put up a lean-to. It wasn't that far from his cabin but he didn't want to miss her in case she was early. That would've been embarrassing. And if she was late, well, that would just prove his steadfastness, waiting for her right on the bank like that.

The canoe wasn't difficult to spot. It was late in the afternoon when it came into view. It tied up right by the lean-to. The paddlers went looking for a pig to roast. Amelia Earhart was in high spirits and she undressed quickly and jumped into the creek and splashed around. Your father tossed her the bar of soap and the shampoo she'd asked for in the cable and then turned away so he wouldn't sully his name by acting like a voyeur. He had a new dress for her too, from J.C. Penney. She'd given him her size and color preference.

My father bought a dress at J.C. Penney for Amelia Earhart?

He did. It fit a little loose because she was undernourished from the long boat trip but she still looked fabulous in it. Ravishing. Heading over to the diner, she said she felt like a new woman. And looked like one too. No one recognized her here. Your father merely told people she was a distant relative from out of state.

He'd picked up some sleepwear for her too, on the modest side, and he let her have his bed and he slept on a cot. He'd improvised a partition between them in the cabin. Being kin, there could be no fooling around. They went through all the notes he'd compiled searching for his own roots and through all the records he'd previously gone through in the courthouse and the town hall and the churches. Until there were no notes and no records left to go through again. But they couldn't find a connection.

And then it came to her that she'd got it wrong. It must have been McSweeney blood she had in her, not FitzSweeney. Additional research pointed to a Hawaiian clan of McSweeneys that had settled on Maui. Ironically, she wasn't that far from Maui when she was rescued with or in the canoe. Some might say she'd been outriggered many thousands of miles away from there for nothing. But nothing's for nothing. Your father convinced her they should make up for lost time now that they weren't related. And make up for lost time they did.

Their tête-à-tête?

A sizzler! Night and day! A wonder the cabin didn't catch on fire. They knew it would have to end eventually and neither of them had regrets when it did. They parted on the best of terms. A farewell breakfast at the diner and a big kiss and a long hug and Amelia Earhart walked out Main Street to the edge of town, stuck out her thumb, and began hitchhiking to California. She sent Fitz a postcard from San Francisco, letting him know that she'd obtained passage on a steamer to Maui. Another postcard, from Maui, that she was pregnant. And another when the baby was born. She named him Sweeney. Sweeney Earhart.

I've a half-brother named Sweeney Earhart?

Well, yes. Amelia kept in touch with your father right along, while he was still here in Saint Plato, then in Saskatchewan after he fled there. The Maui McSweeneys seemed to have died out so she found a little place in the hills upcountry and

149

raised the kid and kept to herself.

He would've been an only child, like me.

True. And like you he got a girl pregnant. In his case in a pineapple grove. The girl's father came after him with a harpoon and the lad made sure he got to the church on time. They had a baby girl and named her Denise and, uh, the new waitress at the diner? She's *that* Denise. She's Denise Earhart. She's your father's granddaughter.

She's—?

I've been meaning to tell her.

If she's my father's granddaughter, I'm her, uh, I'm her—

It's a twister all right. But no question you're, um—how should I phrase it?

*

In a bubbly party mood, Denise Earhart squeals into the house before Silas can decide how to phrase it. She finds Molly and they hug and Molly pours her a tumbler of Veezlaat and brings her into the living room and over to the love seat and formally introduces her and Dennis to each other.

Well, I've got to scoot, Silas mumbles, getting up from the love seat as the introducing wanes. He proceeds to scoot.

Molly scoots too.

Denise is svelte and sexy and does look like Ellen Barkin in *The Big Easy*. She takes a sip of the Veezlaat, hands the tumbler to Dennis, lifts Sebastian from his lap, waking the cat, tumbles onto Dennis's lap herself, and puts Sebastian on hers.

*Irrrph-iphrrph.*

Mmmm, Denise says, nuzzling Dennis's neck. What a day! Shooting down the drone! And all those chestnuts! And all those monks!

I—

Sebastian hops off Denise's lap, flops down where Silas was sitting, and starts washing himself.

Dennis stares blankly at some faraway invisible spot.

I—

He can't immediately get beyond *I*.

Oh, Denny! I was joking about the monks! Denise says. I *have* saved myself for you! She French kisses his ear.

I—

Let's go upstairs, she whispers.

He gulps down the Veezlaat, the whole tumblerful at once. We can't, he says.

Why ever not?

Uh, because we're, uh, I mean, uh, there's something I, something I—

Something you *what*, Denny?

Sebastian looks up from his washing.

Something I, uh, need to, that is, something you need to, uh, know about, about my, uh, my parentage and—

Oh, I know all about that.

You know about—?

Brother Zeke told me.

Sebastian goes back to his washing.

Brother Zeke?

Yeah, at the abbey while the chestnuts were roasting. He said he got to know you pretty well when you were a monk and—

But I was never—

And that you're biracial.

Huh?

That your father was a Chinese laundryman—

That's not—

And your mother was very dark.

Uh, not in the sense—

None of it matters, Denny. Nor that you used to siesta with a consecrated virgin. That's kinda impressive actually.

But—

So can we go upstairs now?

*author photo: Steve Lee*

David Simms set foot in this particular world during the first half of the last century. He didn't get around to fiction until the start of the current one. Before that, he did many things. His previous novel, *The Stars of Axuncanny,* also was published by Livingston Press. Now and then poetry of his has appeared here and there. He once lived in New Jersey.

Printed and bound by PG in the USA

USA2018PGIL